THE CRY OF THE SLOTH

THE CRY OF THE SLOTH

*The Mostly Tragic Story of Andrew Whittaker
Being His Collected, Final,
and Absolutely Complete Writings*

BY SAM SAVAGE

COFFEE HOUSE PRESS

MINNEAPOLIS :: 2009

FIC

COFFEE HOUSE PRESS books are available to the trade
through our primary distributor, Consortium Book Sales
& Distribution, www.cbsd.com or (800) 283-3572. For
personal orders, catalogs, or other information, write to:
info@coffeehousepress.org.

Coffee House Press is a nonprofit literary publishing
house. Support from private foundations, corporate giving
programs, government programs, and generous individuals helps make the publication of our books possible. We
gratefully acknowledge their support in detail in the back
of this book.

To you and our many readers around the world,
we send our thanks for your continuing support.

LIBRARY OF CONGRESS CIP INFORMATION
Savage, Sam, 1940–
The cry of the sloth / by Sam Savage.
p. cm.
ISBN 978-1-56689-231-5 (alk. paper)
1. Middle-aged men—Fiction. 2. Authorship—Fiction.
3. Revenge—Fiction. 4. Psychological fiction. I. Title.
3619.A84C79 2009
PS813'.6—DC22
2009020904
1 3 5 7 9 8 6 4 2
FIRST EDITION | FIRST PRINTING
PRINTED IN THE UNITED STATES

THE CRY OF THE SLOTH

What happens to us
either happens to everyone or only to us:
in the first instance it's banal;
in the second it's incomprehensible.
—FERNANDO PESSOA

JULY

Dear Mr. Fontini,

This is for the record. The sheetrocker has submitted his bill for replacing the ceiling in the kitchen. This was, as you are surely aware, a rather large piece of ceiling, more ceiling, in fact, than many people are unfortunate enough to have in their living rooms. Furthermore, this is the second time, which makes it cumulatively more difficult for me to assume the burden of payment. I am not a wellspring of funds— many people would vouch for that. In short, I cannot remit to the repair people funds in excess of $300 out of my pocket. I enclose a copy of the bill for your perusal. Please remit by the time of your next rent due.

Sincerely yours,
Andrew Whittaker,
The Whittaker Company

¶

Dear Jolie,

This is a smaller check than you expected, and that can't be helped. Never mind what the separation agreement asserts, you know as well as I do the properties are not "income-generating assets." Even at the time of your departure at least half of them were white elephants or worse, and they are now so heavily mortgaged, so *deteriorated,* they barely suffice to keep my small raft afloat while it is being tossed about on an ocean of shit, meager as it is and weighted with the barest of necessities. (I mean to say the raft is meager; the ocean of shit is, of course, boundless.) By "deteriorated" I mean *falling apart.* Mrs. Crumb attempted to open her bedroom window last week and it tumbled out into the street. She's going to have to make do with plastic sheeting, and in the meantime I've had to knock twenty bucks off her rent. There are new vacancies every month, an unstaunchable hemorrhage. Two of the units off Airport Drive remain unrented despite all my work, even though I have ads running constantly. It's ninety-seven degrees outside and I don't dare turn on the air conditioner. The money I am sending now I have siphoned—"diverted" I think is the legal term—from the Repair and Maintenance Fund. You know perfectly well that scrimping there now will only serve to reduce revenues in the future. I recommend you think about that. If Todd Fender calls me I will hang up.

They've taken down the big elm tree across the street. It was the last elm on the block. After the sawyers left I went over and stood on the broad white stump and stared across at our house, in the sun and heat, without the mercy of shadows. I was struck by how uninteresting it looks.

The word seems to be out. People have stopped asking me about you and how I'm getting along. Instead, I get looks of silent commiseration, in which I bask. And when I walk, I swing my arms in a manner I take to be jaunty—that's to confuse and confound them. In the old days I would have carried an ivory-pommeled cane and people seeing me would have said, "There goes that literary gent." But now they say . . . Well, what *do* they say?

Affectionately,
Andy

¶

BIG AND COZY! 1730 Airport Drive. Duplex. Both units 2 bdrm 1 bath. Appliances. New paint and carpet. Spacious older-type bldg with many upgrades. Top unit has view of small pond. Centrally located minutes from bus line. $125 + utils.

¶

Dear Marcus,

I count on my fingers, can it really have been eleven years? We promised to keep in touch, and yet . . . I suppose even "out East" you now and then get wind of our doings back here in Rapid Falls. I for my part have needed only the Sunday supplement of our local *Current* to keep abreast of *your* career. (I chuckle aloud as I write this, remembering how "career" was once a dirty word to our little band of roughnecks; a chuckle tinged with melancholy). They once published a photo of you on your motorcycle. That was certainly a handsome machine; I never saw so much chrome. At the time I considered sending the picture on to you, but was prevented by the thought that you probably have a clipping service. Each time I see your name in print, dear Marcus, or catch a "rave review" of yet another novel, I experience a salience of warm pleasure at the spectacle of an old pal succeeding, a pleasure mingled, I confess, with a small measure of personal satisfaction. And why should it not be? It was I, after all, who led our little gang in those experiments that you and others, including the wily Willy, have honed to such perfection. I think of myself as the spark that lit the conflagration. It's a pity the idea of directly importing movie characters into the novel has become so vitiated by practitioners of lesser talents than you. Must we count poor Willy among them? I fear for him.

But stay. I am not writing to talk old shop, nor indeed (if I may turn a phrase), to shop old gossip. I have a friend in need. Not a friend of flesh and blood, though I have those as well perforce. I allude to *Soap: A Journal of the Arts*, the little literary review of which I am founder and editor, with its annual supplements, *Soap Express* and *The Best of Soap*. I imagine you have heard talk of us in the smaller press, though you might not have been aware of my connection (I don't blazon my name across the cover), and you might even have seen the mention in *American Aspects* a few years back, in a review of Troy Sokal's *Moon Light and Moon Dark*, where they contrasted—favorably— *Soap*'s "neomodernist shibboleths" with the "murky enthusiasms" of Sokal's "smut and manure movement." Naturally they got almost everything wrong: there is no rivalry between *Soap* and Sokal, and S & M is a "movement" only in Sokal's imagination. I did send you some early copies of the mag, which you did not acknowledge. Perhaps you never got them.

Permit me to lay out a few of our "firsts." We were the first to publish Sarah Burkett's harrowing travelogue *The Toilets of Annapurna* as well as excerpts from Rolf Keppel's Zen novel *Ball Bearings*. Both were later republished by big New York houses to no small acclaim. I am sure you know the titles even if you have not read the books. (I am sorry to say that a reader would have to scrutinize the microscopic print on the copyright page to learn of our role in bringing those authors to light in the first place, both being basically small-town nobodies and with manners that show it.) Miriam Wildercamp's mirror poetry appeared regularly in our pages at a time when no one else would touch it. Our newest discovery is Dahlberg Stint, who I expect will soon be making waves coast to coast. All this in addition to my own stories, reviews, and occasional short poems. I have edited the mag practically singlehandedly for, lo, these seven years. During that time I have pushed hard against a deadening complacency, striving with Poundian fury to establish some minimal standards. I am proud to say that we now and then have managed to shake things up in a positive way.

But obviously an enterprise like *Soap* cannot survive on subscriptions alone. I have had to rob countless hours from my own writing and go about hat in hand in pursuit of public and private grants. It was never enough, and we have been able to survive only through handouts from my own personal funds. Jolie and I even held regular bake sales on the University Mall, and that worked well for a time, but since then I have lost her assistance, not just her baking skills but also her typing and bookkeeping. Two years ago she moved to New York, to Brooklyn, to study theater, even though she had never shown any interest in theater before. In the meantime relations with the local "arts people" have gone very sour, perhaps in part because I no longer have Jolie's sparkling personality running interference for me. I do have a tendency, I fear, to speak my mind. But I think the root of the problem is that it has gradually dawned upon these people that I am not going to let *Soap* become a dumping ground for their mediocre productions. Things have come to such a pass that *The Art News* feels entitled to regularly mock the journal in their "Monthly Roundup," referring to it as *"Soup"* and *"Sap"* and other imbecilic permutations, *"Pus"* and *"Glop."* That alone should tell you what we are up against. I do sometimes envy you in New York.

With the economy what it is—and the apparent incapacity of the Nixon people to do anything about it—my personal income has shrunk, indeed it has shriveled, while expenses have swelled. Unless I take strong steps, *Soap* is going to become permanently derailed. And more bake sales are not going to cut it. Which, dear Marcus, brings me to the point of this all-too-rambling letter. I have something big in mind for next spring. Plans are still sketchy, but I see a kind of symposium cum retreat cum workshop cum writer's colony sometime in April, just as the daffodils appear. The idea is to bring first-rate talents from around the region together with a paying audience for a weekend of workshops and lectures. As you know, the sort of people who attend these things are not usually terribly well informed about who is who in the literary world (most have probably never even heard of Chester Sill, or Mitsy Collingwood, who have both promised to be there), so it would be a tremendous boost to have at least one "national figure." And I must say, after the brouhaha around *The Secret Life of Echoes* you are certainly that! So will you come? Along with a resounding "Yes," I hope you will send along any bright ideas you might have for the program. Nothing is set in stone yet.

Your old pal,

Andrew Whittaker

p.s. I regret that neither the mag nor I will likely be able to pay you for your time or even reimburse travel expenses. I feel bad about that. You will, however, find commodious lodging at my house, and when the crowds have dwindled, some good company for late night talk. I know I'll not scare you away when I say that I look forward to "taking the gloves off" in regard to some of your recent work.

¶

Disgusting, disgusting. Lying, sycophantic, stupid. The ingratiating phrases. How can I be so loathsome? What I need is a door I can walk through and get out of the world for a while. When I was a child I liked to hide in the big closet in my parents' bedroom, curl up in the dark with the smell of mothballs and the feeling of sitting on the lumps that were Mama's shoes.

¶

Dear Mrs. Brud,

Seven months, and I have had no rent payment from you. Twice I have sent courteous reminders. Those did not scold, neither did they speak of breach of contract or invoke harsh specters of legal action and ignominious eviction. In view of that you can picture my surprise when I opened your reply this morning and out fell no check or postal money order. What fluttered to the floor instead was your astonishing letter. Madame: permit me to recall the circumstance of our discussion when you came to my house five months ago, you being at the time two months in arrears. You were distressed, distraught even, and as I am not a Scrooge or heartless rack-renter, I did not leave you standing on the doorstep in the rain; I invited you in, offered you a seat. All chairs being occupied by my books and papers, we were forced to share the small portion of the sofa that was still free. You were wet and trembling with cold; I brought you a martini and some peanuts. I listened patiently to the story of your husband's accident with the electric blender and the medical expenses arising from that, and your son's wrongful arrest and the legal expenses arising from that. I was moved to utter the platitudes of sympathy usual in such cases. However, when I told you not to worry, it did not cross the purlieus of my mind that you would construe this as carte blanche to live rent-free forever. As to your current letter, I do not understand what you intend when you assert that if I insist on the back rent you will be "forced to tell my husband." Tell him *what*? That the legal owner of the house in which you reside would like some meager imbursement? And what do you mean by the phrase "if you want to see me again." What *are* you suggesting? You wept. You were sitting on *my* sofa. It was *perfectly normal* that I should find that distressing in the extreme. I held you in my arms as I would hold a weeping child. I muttered "there, there." If I let myself stroke your head and sweep with ink-stained finger a sodden strand of graying hair from your lips— after you had, as it were, fallen over on me—it was without any (dare I say it?) *sexual* interest. I merely hoped those gestures would lend some credence to my words of sympathy, which will, should such an event recur in the future, I assure you, be entirely pro forma. Please remit 7 x 130 = $910.

Yours sincerely,
Andrew Whittaker
The Whittaker Company

¶

Dear Contributor,

Thank you for giving us the opportunity to read your work. After careful consideration, we have reluctantly concluded that it does not meet our needs at this time.

The Editors at *Soap*

¶

Dear Jolie,

Why did I never wonder about what was happening to Papa? There he was, blood pressure so high it made him bug-eyed, a malady of the skin on his back and buttocks so itchy he would stand in the kitchen and furiously scratch with a metal spatula until his shirt was streaked with blood, and a tendency to drink himself stuporous at supper. Mama would try to snatch the plate away the instant she saw him nodding, but sometimes he'd go face down in the meatloaf and potatoes or whatever she had fixed that night, applesauce and pork chops, before she could reach it, though more often he went off the chair sideways. It never even occurred to me that this sad comedy bore any relation to what he did all day, what he was *forced* to do all day. I just took it as the natural course of the man's life. And now it's happening to me. I mean *that life* is happening to me. One day I'm out dunning tenants for back rent, hearing their sob stories, listening glassy-eyed to the whine of complaints about stopped drains and unkillable mice and furnaces that won't heat and ceilings that have fallen down. I'll never understand these people. Do they strip to their underwear just for the purpose of answering the doorbell? Or is it so they can more ostentatiously scratch while I am speaking? Next day I am on the phone trying to wheedle some tradesman into working for credit. And then when I do find somebody, he screws the work up so badly I have to go back and do it over myself, even though I don't know how, but at least I work cheap. How about that for my epitaph: *He worked cheap.* And then when the damn thing breaks again they call me up and *threaten*. I'll end up carrying a pistol around with me like Papa. Then there are the big boys—the banks, the water works, the electric company, the

9

phone company, especially the phone company. I have dreams in which I am pursued by men in armor. Sometimes I frighten myself with the thought that any minute I am going to descend howling into the street. Or maybe take Papa's pistol, push calmly through the glass doors of some downtown office, and *Bang! Bangety bang bang!* Things go on like this for weeks at a time, until I'm utterly exhausted. No psoriasis yet, my head still floats bravely above my plate of fried Spam, but I'm depleted, drained, spent. When I finally get home, I have to lie down on the sofa, chest heaving as after some huge physical exertion. You might give me a call sometime.

Andy

¶

ENJOY A FAMILY LIFESTYLE! 73 Charles Court. Unique single-family bungalow-style house in desirable neighborhood. 2 bdrm 1 bath. Large closets. Security fence. Paved yard. Lighted parking. 10-min walk to shops and gas station. $155 + utils.

¶

Dear Mama,

I hope this letter finds you recovered. It's true, colds can be very unpleasant, and it was not kind of Elaine to make fun of you or take away your Kleenex, if that is really what happened. And despite what you imply, I do know that hedges can be boring when they are all one has to look at. But I am convinced that if you look at them closely and try to see each leaf separately and not just as one among many, you will find them more varied than you thought and interesting enough to make your afternoons pass pleasantly by. I have always believed the reason people are bored is that they don't pay attention to details. I had hoped to race up this month, but I am afraid the Chevy is once again on the fritz. There seems to be something wrong with the radiator, or the transmission, and with the terribly hot weather we're having here it wants to "boil over" even on short trips to the Safeway. I asked Clara about your hair dryer; she says she doesn't remember it. When I'm able to make it, I'll take you out driving. We can scoot over to Woodhaven and visit Winston's tomb; I know you enjoy that, and of course so do I. And by the way, it was unjust of you to say that I "never gave a tin shit" about Winston. In fact, I spoke to Reverend Studfish just last week. He promised he would look into the question, though he did warn me right off the bat that church law seems fairly canonical on the issue. However, I don't think you should let that discourage you, as he never cared for Winston after what he did at Peg's wedding, what he, Winston, did. If it is any comfort to you, I am personally convinced that Winston is happy where he is, wherever that might be.

Much love,
Andy

¶

My very first memory is of Mama brushing her hair. It was a dry evening and in the arid gloaming I could see little sparks leaping between brush and hair like fleas. Bright fleas. It was my first inkling of the role electricity plays in our lives. My earliest memory is of Mama's hand. It was alabaster. It was pale and blue-veined. It was a delicate blue-veined hand bespeaking aristocracy. I lay in my lace-draped bassinet on the porch. She was talking on the phone—to whom I wonder?—and she was saying (I remember the words clearly, though of course it was many months before I developed a vocabulary large enough to understand their meaning, and until that time I could only con them mutely to myself in meaningless incantation): "Send up a chuck roast and some potatoes, two pounds of asparagus, a quart of milk, and a box of Tide." I think back on this memory often, and I marvel how people were once able to order groceries by phone Shit shit shit

¶

Dear Mr. Poltavski,

In response to your request for submission guidelines, I enclose our standard statement. I wish more people would ask for our guidelines before submitting inappropriate material that wastes my time as well as theirs. And thank you for including a stamped return envelope, which not enough of you do either.

A. Whittaker, Editor

¶

GUIDELINES FOR SUBMISSION

Soap is in a national journal devoted to all forms of literary art, including short fiction, poetry, essays, and reviews. We publish six regular issues a year, plus two annual anthologies.

Our contributors include established writers of international reputation as well as talented newcomers. Though we are always happy to see artists breaking new ground, whether in content or in form, we do not have any criteria for publication other than literary excellence. In the current acerbic climate of American letters, with unrestrained emotional outbursts on the one side (the remains of the so-called Beat movement) and amorphous piles of pseudomodernist gibberish on the other, *Soap* steers a middle course. We do not publish devotional materials, greeting card verses, or anything embroidered on cloth. While satire is welcome, the rule for personal invective is KEEP IT CLEAN. Obscenity is tolerated but must not be hurled in the direction of anyone still alive. Originality is a requirement. Characters must not be named K or X. Manifestos must advocate positions no one has ever heard of. We do not publish works in any language but English. While foreign phrases may be sprinkled here and there, a whole lot of that will result in your work being rejected as pretentious trash. All submissions must be typed and double-spaced. Multipage works must be numbered. Contributors are rewarded with two free copies and a twenty percent discount on any additional copies. Submitters should heed the two cardinal rules of carefree publishing. Cardinal Rule #1: DO NOT SEND YOUR ONLY COPY. Cardinal Rule #2: INCLUDE A STAMPED SELF-ADDRESSED RETURN ENVELOPE. A simultaneous violation of both rules will be punished by the utter obliteration of your work.

¶

Dear Mrs. Lessep,

Thanks for letting us read, once again, "The Mistletoe's Little Shoes." After careful consideration, we have concluded that this work still does not meet our needs. I am sorry you were misled by the phrase "does not meet our needs at this time" into thinking you should submit it again. In the publishing world "at this time" really means "forever."

A. Whittaker,
Editor at *Soap*

¶

Dear Mr. Carmichael,

Old people can be difficult, as you must know, and yet they have to be treated kindly, as they are still people. And of course you and I would like to be treated kindly when we become old, as we surely must, even if we end up belonging to that class of unpleasant old persons who are constantly complaining. We are led by natural human impulse to always blame the complainers, just because they are so annoying, without looking deeper into the matter. I say this in order to explain to myself why, since my mother has apparently spoken to you personally about her problems with the attendant Elaine Robinson more than once, no remedy has been forthcoming. This is not right. But rather than joining the list of annoying complainers myself, I thought I would lay out the facts and let you be the judge.

Elaine came to work at Old Ivy Glen shortly after Christmas last year, replacing Dotty. My mother welcomed the change at first, since Dotty had passed most of her shifts droning on about things that not even a lonely bedridden old lady could possibly find interesting. As a consequence, my mother spent much of her first year at Old Ivy Glen pretending to be asleep. Enter Elaine Robinson: big-bosomed and cheerful, with the happy-go-lucky outlook on life that we all find so refreshing in her people. My mother comes from a prominent old Southern family, and she has always felt very close to Negroes of all kinds, and at first she and Elaine seemed to "hit it off." I vividly remember walking down the hall toward Mother's room during one of my monthly visits and overhearing the two of them in warm conversation, Elaine's earthy laughter churning beneath the trills and runs of Mama's little cackles, a slow river, as it were, burbling beneath a mountain brook. My heart leaped, and I exhaled a silent "thank you" to Old Ivy Glen.

Alas, like so many good things, this joy was premature. Those early sprouts of friendship, if that is what they were, were destined to wither in April, when Mama's mind began to wander. She migrated, figuratively speaking, into the storied past, imagining that she was a child in Georgia in slave times, that Old Ivy Glen was her dear old Oakwood restored to its former glory, that Winston, her old Labrador, was a puppy again, and that Elaine was her beloved Feena, the devoted female servant who had helped raise her in later, sadder times, when the family could scarcely pay the light bill, much less Feena, who was content with a small room and cornbread.

One might expect that a nursing professional like Elaine would redouble her sympathy at such moments, that she might indeed take pleasure in joining an old lady on her harmless time-travels, get a kick out of playing a role in these really rather charming fantasies about "the days that are no more." But no! I vividly recall the moment when I realized that the tide of friendship at which I had earlier rejoiced had sunk to a dangerously low ebb. I was sitting with Mama in her room, not talking, but sharing a few minutes of quiet communion, when Elaine and another dark girl came bustling in to change the bedding, laughing and chatting in loud voices about God knows what. This sudden interruption of our communion provoked Mama to open her eyes wide and, seeing the two women standing at the foot of her bed, no doubt dimly, since she was not wearing her glasses, to observe that "there sure are a lot of Feenas around here." I thought this was very funny. Yet I saw right away that Mrs. Robinson was going to let hypersensitiveness spoil the joke for her. I fear I inadvertently made matters worse by continuing to laugh despite her scowling expression.

Since that day I have received reports that Elaine is "getting even" with Mama, tormenting her in numerous aggravating ways. I recognize that some of Mama's complaints are evident exaggerations. None of us think it plausible that Elaine has let hundreds of rats loose in Mama's room. And even if she had, how could she have made them disappear in the morning? But still, I think we cannot be too careful where fragile old people are concerned. I am not at this time demanding the dismissal of Mrs. Robinson. I ask merely that you keep an eye peeled and make *qui vive* your motto.

With filial concern,

A. Whittaker

¶

Dear Vikki,

I've read your latest batch, only wish I could print all eight of them. Since that ain't possible, I want to use "Sally at the Pump," "Calypso," and "Needles and Pins." Lots of terrific stuff in the mailbox lately, stuff I just couldn't turn down. As a result, the mag is way overbooked and I can't work yours in before next summer, at the earliest. Sorry about that and I promise and hope to die no hard feelings here should you want to try someplace else. Overbooked and underfunded—that's it in a nutshell. The result of the last mail appeal was, frankly, disappointing in the extreme. I know everybody is thoroughly fed up by now with my pleas for handouts, so I'm all the more grateful to the handful of loyalists like you and Chumley and a few others who have stuck by me over the years. I've put so much blood and treasure into the magazine, when it hits a rough patch I get just frantic. With the two of you gone, and Jolie gone, I'm more isolated than ever down here. The fact is I'm unspeakably lonely at times. Things have gotten much worse between me and Fran and the swarm of toadies at *The Art News*. We don't even *pretend* anymore. When I cross one of them in the street, he or she (in fact, it's always she) looks the other direction. I love the way their ponytails flick to the side when they jerk their heads around so as not to look at me. I usually send a raspberry after them when they do that. Sometimes they answer by swinging their hips in an exaggerated manner as they stump off, a female gesture that, I must confess, I have never understood. Do you? All this would be just laughable if it were not so infuriating. And of course, aside from not inviting me to their parties, thank God for that, they're doing everything in their power to prevent my symposium project from ever getting off the ground. I have it on good authority that Fran referred to it at an Arts Council Grant Committee meeting as "Andy's aberration"—she's going to make damn sure I don't get one red penny from them. The *Rapid Falls Current* ran an article last week on the local scene. They didn't even bother to contact me. I'd love to just forget the whole business, take a couple of weeks off, and drive up and visit you two. But with money this tight, plus a million things to do here, there's no way I can swing it. I'm forty-three years old. I'm not supposed to be doing this. Give Chumley a punch in the snout from me, and tell him to send me some photos of the stuff he's doing.

Missing you both,
Andy

¶

Dear Mr. Freewinder,

Yes, I did receive your earlier letter, and I want you to know that we are, as you suggested, taking vigorous steps, that I personally am taking them. Indeed, things are happening even as I write. This may not be apparent, since they are happening mostly behind the scenes, so to speak, and in small increments, little bits at a time, which are nevertheless accumulating. It is true that The Whittaker Company has hit a rough patch. The problem can be traced to an unusually long run of low-quality tenants, and not to my casual management style, as you describe it. I am working vigorously to root those low-quality ones out and to get better-quality ones in. As you can well imagine, this is difficult to bring off as long as the poor-quality ones are still there, sitting on the steps in their undershirts. It will take time. We are upgrading

18

at every turn. If you can persuade American Midlands to suspend the loan repayments for a few months, you will all be
pleasantly surprised.

Sincerely,

Andrew Whittaker

The Whittaker Company

¶

Dear Mr. Goodall,

Thanks for letting us read your collection of poems
"Swinging the Mattock." After careful consideration, we have
reluctantly concluded that the work does not meet our needs
at this time.

Andrew Whittaker, Editor

¶

If I could see myself clearly for one moment; even in the mirror. One day I behold there an imposing man of considerable
dignity. He ought to sport a gray fedora, but I don't have one
for him. Of course he would not wear a hat indoors anyway,
unless he happened to be a policeman. If he were a policeman,
it would be some kind of detective, homicide probably. I love
the way he shrugs. They say, "we love his slow shrug." That
shrug is a perfect mingling of confidence and disdain, with just
a smidgen of despair. He is not the kind of man to use a phrase
like "smidgen of despair," though. He would not say "smidgen"
or "despair," and certainly not both together. What if he wanted
to put a little something in something? He wouldn't cook, so it
couldn't be salt, though if he did he would say "dash."

And sometimes I see a different man, one who is not imposing but lumbering, bloated; I want to say he is *receding*. I notice how his cheeks puff out. He doesn't seem to have a definite shape, or the shape has blurred edges. He is not clever with his hands, I am sure of that. He is always breaking things, like lockets that people have asked him to fix. He snaps the delicate gold chain, and the locket slips off and gets lost down a heat vent; it contains her only picture of her grandmother. His piano teacher called him sausage fingers. He doesn't have a hat either, though he ought to wear one, because his hair is thinning; under the fluorescent light in the room with the mirror his scalp is blue-gray and scaly. In the case of the first man, words like "adamantine" and "steely" come to mind. In the case of the second, the words are "gooey," or maybe "runny" and "amorphous." His—or their—jaw "juts" on the one hand, "hangs" on the other. A man without qualities. I remember Jolie saying she would never marry anybody as *ambiguous* as I am.

¶

Dear Dahlberg,

A note to let you know that the larcenous literary postman who you feared had made off with your MS has apparently had a change of heart. It arrived this afternoon, battered but intact. I had not expected anything quite so *huge*; we might have to spread it out over several numbers. I can't look at it now, as I'm on my way out. Just want you to know I have it and am looking forward to reading it.

Andy

¶

PLACE ALL TRASH IN METAL RECEPTACLES LOCATED AT THE BACK
OF THE BUILDING

¶

Dear Mr. Stumphill,

Thank you for giving us the opportunity to read your work. The story has some fine parts, though it is much too long, not just for our magazine but for most readers not familiar with apiculture. The bees have a lot of personality, but there are too many of them and their names are confusing. The murder, while gruesome, is not plausible, since how could the bees know which brother had taken the shirt? Bob Curry lives up your way. If you run into him, transmit my greetings.

Sincerely,

A. Whittaker, Editor

¶

Dear Sirs,

This morning I woke to discover that my telephone is no longer making a friendly buzzing sound when I press it to my ear. It makes no sound at all, and that is a VERY BAD THING. I am aware of the sum I owe you, I do not dispute the legitimacy of your case. Whenever I could I have sent little sums which were more than pocket change. I have showed good faith. I have a business to run. It may not look like a business to you, but it is one to me. If it is not advertised in the yellow pages that is only because I could not AFFORD to advertise it in the yellow pages. You should have thought of that. I explained to Mrs. Slippert in person that if she cut off my

21

phone I would probably NEVER be in a position to pay you. That was an appeal to your self-interest, and the fact that it had no effect rebounds to your credit. So now I appeal to your heart. I am on my knees. This is painful to my pride. PLEASE restore my service. Six more months and I will pay you in full. You have my word on that.

Very sincerely,

Andrew W. Whittaker

¶

DO NOT THROW CIGARETTE BUTTS IN FLOWER POTS

¶

Dear Fern Moss,

After careful consideration the staff at *Soap* has reluctantly concluded that your poems are not a good fit for us at this time. However, I don't feel comfortable returning them to you with only a rejection slip for company. While we endeavor to make these rejections as short and painless as possible, we were all young writers once and know from personal experience the deep wounds they can cause, wounds which in some cases fester for years unseen, only to burst drunkenly forth at someone's publication party later. Your work has a bold freshness I would hate to see squelched by a thoughtless act of ours.

I want to say right off the bat that I am surprised Mr. Crawford recommended a journal like *Soap* as the best place for you to start, though that is certainly testimony to his high opinion of your efforts. Am I wrong in assuming that you have in fact never examined a copy of our publication? Frankly, I fear you would find most of the things we publish quite depressing, if not downright baffling. Some of it you might find offensive. This of course, while regrettable, cannot be helped.

That said, I consider your series "Self Portrait in Five" to be exceptional work for someone so young. Mr. Crawford is certainly right that it has "sparkle," and you deserve all the A's he can give you. While the poems are not the sort of thing *Soap* normally publishes, they have genuine poetic energy and real charm. I believe the ones that mention horses would have a good chance of acceptance at *Corral* or *American Pony*. My dentist carries both magazines, and I have noticed they regularly publish verse on equine themes, most of it inferior to yours. And there is nothing wrong with starting out small. You make a reputation there and then you move on. That's how we all did it.

I am only too aware how painful it is to have one's work rejected. It is most painful the first time it happens, before one has acquired the requisite carapace of cynicism. For that reason I want to insist that I see genuine potential in your work. I am truly sorry that we can't use your submission this time. We will of course be happy to consider your work in the future, though I recommend you familiarize yourself with the sort of writing we publish before sending along anything else.

Best wishes,

A. Whittaker, Editor at *Soap*

¶

Egan Phillips stood on the front porch looking out over the turgid water of Lake Michigan. A yellow cardigan caused him to stand out against the grayness of the day and to be noticed by a woman on a bicycle. She biked this way every day to take milk to an old woman, biked past this house. In fact, she had biked past it from time to time since she was a child, when she had also driven past it with her father on a tractor. He let her ride on the tractor when he thought her mother would not find out. This was a secret between them. She was surprised to see someone standing on the porch, since the house was scarcely better than a ruin. Something about the figure in the yellow cardigan, something dark, caused her to put out her feet, and sliding them on the gravel on the roadside, to come to a complete halt in front of the house, though safely on the opposite side of the road, for she did not know what the figure might portend. The man on the porch noticed how she stopped by sliding her feet on the gravel, and it reminded him of someone long ago. The wind was blowing yellow strands of blond hair across her face. Now this girl, silhouetted against the heaving breast of the tumid lake, hallooed in his direction.

¶

To All Tenants:

As specified in your contracts, rent is due on the first business day of each month. This means it is due *in my office* on that day. Being somewhere in the postal system does not count. Beginning August 1, a surcharge of two dollars ($2.00) will be added to the subsequent month's rent for *each day* your rent is late.

The Management

¶

Dear Willy,

I count on my fingers, can it really have been eleven years? We promised to keep in touch, and yet . . . I suppose even in California you now and then get wind of our doings back here, things that people in your area would be interested in if they could get over certain regional myopias of their own. But of course you know that. I snap up your books the day they appear. Well, "snap up" is probably not the word, since they don't exactly "appear" here; I have to order them from New York, which I do the moment I learn a new one is out, which is sometimes months later. And now and then I catch a review of one of them in some small periodical. I myself wrote a very positive little essay on your third novel for *The Glass Stopper*—an interesting little mag while it lasted. Unfortunately the guy who was putting it out killed himself before the issue containing my article could appear; he jumped off the roof of a parking garage in front of a bus. Otherwise I would have sent it on to you. In that essay I argued that *Cadillac Waltz, Buttocks,* and especially *Elevator Ping-Pong Raga* belong right up there with Simon Kershmeyer's best stuff. I can probably dig up a carbon if you are interested. Each time I see a favorable mention of your work I experience a salience of warm pleasure at the spectacle of an old friend doing well, a pleasure mingled, I confess, with a small measure of personal satisfaction. And why should it not be? It was I after all who led our little group in those experiments which you especially have honed to such perfection. I like to think of myself as the spark that lit the conflagration. By the same token, I am thoroughly exasperated by the denigration of your last novel in the *New York Times*, the *New Yorker*, *Harper's*, the *Saturday Review*, etc., especially when I consider the deference those same people pay to that buffoon Marcus Quiller, from whom oddly enough I received a card just last week. I'm happy to report that he is as he was: smug, affable, and looking out for Number One.

But enough of that; I am not writing to shop old gossip. I have a friend in need, a very special kind of friend made all of words and paper. I allude, of course, to good old *Soap*. I can't imagine you haven't run across my magazine out there, though you might not have been aware of my intimate connection; I don't blazon my name across the cover. We have a couple of outlets in your area, and one can usually pick up a copy at one of them, but just in case, I'm enclosing our last issue. I'm afraid it is a little difficult to read, since some of the pages were printed out of order. It might be easier to tear out the staples first. They also forgot the page numbers, but I have penciled those in for you. I am one of the founders of the journal (my ex-wife Jolie was the other), and I have been the sole editor for lo these seven years. No one who has seen any of the recent issues, among our strongest, could possibly surmise the painful truth—that the magazine is, if not on its deathbed, then staggering dangerously toward it. Unless it receives a transfusion of real money soon it will certainly expire. (But don't worry, I'm not asking you for *that* sort of help). The demise of *Soap* would not be of great moment to anyone but me and a few hundred loyal subscribers and contributors except for the fact that there is *absolutely nothing* to take its place. Imagine: a region the size of France and not a single venue for first-class work by local writers. For seven years, beginning with our first issue of just three mimeographed pages, I have striven with Poundian fury to put work of that caliber in front of the public, and I've done this not simply without the *support* of our local so-called art leaders but in the face of their active *opposition*. (I say opposition rather than sabotage only because I have no material proof.) Without *Soap*'s voice—however shrill it may sound sometimes to some people—the entire region would be defined by the vulgar populism of works like Sokal's *Moon Light and Moon Dark*, a depressing example if there ever was one of the sort of book esteemed here today. But of course, having grown up here, you know all about that. And yet we keep on going, you and I. And for me, besides the slow insect-like construction of my own works—I am currently laboring on an odd little something which I suppose we'll have to call a novel—keeping on means keeping *Soap* afloat.

Racking my brains, I have come up with an idea for next April or May that I think will turn the trick, generate the needed funds, and at the same time land us on the map of public opinion. *Soap* is going to host a weekend of symposiums, lectures, workshops, and readings. The idea is to take real avant-garde literary works and under the slogan "Far Out is Fun" fling them like gauntlets in the face of an astonished public. In the same spirit, I am thinking of inviting street performers to come in during the breaks, and maybe also at mealtimes, or does that seem to you over the top? We don't want anything that might drown out the discussions, which I anticipate will be lively and contentious, so maybe just fire-eaters, jugglers, and the like, and no musicians unless it's some barely audible ones off in a corner, harpists and such. I've been working to come up with a name for the event. How does "The Words on Fire National Conference" strike you? Is that just too flat? And do you think "Festival" would be better than "Conference"? I go back and forth on that one. I want to suggest a celebratory spirit, but I don't want it to sound like a big party. I've been talking this thing up locally for a couple of months now, and the response so far has been terrific. Unless I run things on into the wee hours, we are not going to have nearly enough room on the schedule for all the events people have suggested. There is just an *amazing* hunger out there for something like this. A big question still up in the air, though, is the name of the person who will give the Awards Lecture. That lecture, along with the subsequent banquet and formal dance, is going to be the biggest bang of the whole shebang. The downtown Grand Hotel has just refurbished the splendid old Hoover Ballroom, and I'm told a few of our local bands are quite good (I myself hardly ever listen to music). I've had lots of unsuitable suggestions for the speaker, and to those I've responded with only a noncommittal nod. That's because I've had you in mind from the outset but have held the idea close to my chest in case you're booked for that week. I can't pay you in advance, but I can promise a reimbursement of expenses plus a modest honorarium after the event. Your presence will close the festival on an unmistakable note of defiance. Of course our local so-called movers and shakers would prefer a venerable warhorse like Norman Mailer or, even worse, a flash-in-the-pan mountebank like Quiller. I remember how you used to refer to the NYT's best seller list as "the roster of shame" and how, encouraged by our shouts and laughter, you would climb up on a table in the cafeteria and read it aloud each Sunday, pronouncing the titles with that drawling faux-Oxford accent of yours, which would break everybody up, you made all the books sound perfectly ridiculous. So I rather doubt you've read *The Secret Life of Echoes*, Quiller's latest concoction.

Considering the well-known literary penchants of the accused, you'll not be surprised to learn that it's another farrago of soft porn and phony philosophical ruminations; they fuck and then they talk about the Meaning of History. He has Errol Flynn appear as a ghost to give advice on how to dress to the poor working-class slob who through good looks and brains has landed a job at Goldman Sachs. In the cubicle next to his dwells Neenah of the long legs, big boobs, and "moist pudendum" (his words). Need I say more? The armies are ranged for battle. Gird your loins, Willy, and join us in April.

My very best,
Andy Whittaker

¶

Dear Dahlberg,

I've spent the past day and a half on your MS. I wanted to read it all the way through before writing you, but I can't go on. I really don't know *what* to say except it's not what I expected, which was something more in line with your earlier stuff. Reading this new material was like walking on a thick pile of soggy sheetrock. One thinks, after finishing one interminable sentence, with no verb or subject in the offing, and having finally reached the relative safety of a full stop, that one will just not have enough strength for the next sentence, not enough *willpower* to haul a clogged boot out of the sticky mess and heave it forward into yet more mess, until finally one *really can't*, and doesn't, at which point one lets the whole thing slide off one's lap onto the floor.

What happened to the tough little guy who told those tough little stories about his life as a hardware store clerk?

"Good Luck at Smart Value" got more favorable comments than just about anything we've published in years. I think I told you that. Sure, we had predictable penny-ante back-biting from the tiresome yahoos at *The Art News*. I would never have sent you the clipping if it had occurred to me that you would take it as anything but a grand joke. When these people *like* your stuff, Dahl, that's when you better start worrying. Believe me, your description of the owner's wife heaving those fifty-pound sacks of Quikrete into the bed of a pickup was flat-out *amazing*. I mean, *that* was real writing. You could just as well have been describing a reciprocating single-action piston pump with pulse damper or a smoothly ratcheting mechanical windlass, the writing was that cold and dead, and yet it was also feverish. It had the brutal honesty we usually associate with instruction manuals. That you are not exactly a polished writer worked in your favor; it's how Hemingway might have written had he never gone to high school. I confess, I envied your raw energy, the authenticity of that voice, and I thought how fun it would be to write like that. I am reluctantly returning your MS.

Andy

¶

I am just now becoming aware that an odd thing has been happening. Ordinary objects—chairs, tables, trees, my own hands—seem to have become closer than they were. The colors are brighter, the edges sharper. This is a process that has been going on, that has been increasing, over the past several weeks without my quite noticing. And with it has come a tremendous new confidence. Maybe I am finally getting over Jolie's leaving. Looking back, I can see that I have probably been in a real clinical depression. Only now, in retrospect, am I able to see clearly what a solitary time I have had of it, almost never going out to a restaurant, to the movies, anywhere in fact except for walks by myself in the park. I just opened cans at home. And the terrible thing is, after a month or two, I started eating directly out of them, out of the cans, standing in the kitchen and spooning it up and then leaving the cans on the counter. Now the ants have come, millions of them. That sort of behavior feeds on itself. And of course I was not good company, I was terrible company, I can see that now. So after a couple of feeble tries people naturally didn't want to invite me over again, just to watch me sitting around under my cloud of gloom. The idea was, I guess, if I couldn't entertain them, then to hell with me. I started having thoughts that I see now were practically paranoid delusions. I decided our so-called best friends, the Willinghams and the Pretzkys, had never liked me, that it was always only Jolie they wanted to invite and I was only there as some kind of unfortunate appendage, an exceedingly unattractive older relative she was forced to drag around with her. I wonder what they would say now if they could see the ants. On the other hand, how did I behave the few times the Pretzksys did invite me? I sat there moving the food around on my plate. I think I droned, I could hear myself droning, sitting at the end of the table going on and on, but I couldn't stop it, stop myself, the words just pouring out, almost without inflection, in a dull stream. I remember on one occasion glancing up from my plate and seeing Karen dart a meaningful glance at John, who was staring at his own plate. Meaningful, and yet *I could not understand what it meant.* God, how I hated them both when I got home! Hated them for making me look like a bumbling fool, and worse, like a bore. Now I feel a new power to write, the sentences just pouring out. I feel the books in a stack inside me. I have only to open them up, open myself up, and read off the words.

¶

Dear Jolie,

One week despair spreads like mold, and the next week happiness glitters like a bright polish on all the little buttons (I mean the days). Do you remember, after Papa finally died and we got the buildings, how we thought we were set up for life? We were going to be like Leonard and Virginia Woolf, except in reverse—you were going to work the presses, while I was upstairs turning out the novels. Laughable, isn't it? Or maybe it was Sartre and Simone. I look back at that now, at us then, at me and my fantasies and the stack of my aborted efforts, and I grimace.

I was, naturally, overjoyed to hear that "dear Marcus Quiller" was standing on your doorstep when you came home from class last Friday. After all these many years! And that he looked so youthful! I should have known when I let slip you had moved to Brooklyn that he'd hunt you up, or hunt you down, depending on how one looks at it, at him. He doesn't miss a lick, young Marcus. I obviously do not look youthful. I look in the mirror, and I look ravaged, I look hateful. I spend *most* of my time at the most dreary, mind-deadening, soul-killing, gut-twisting activities you can imagine. But of course you *can't* imagine, because it's *far worse* than when you were here. But I'm not writing to complain. I am, in fact, doing quite well, despite everything. My projects are roaring apace. But I'm in a dry patch financially, and you are going to have to make out on your own until I can get things turned around. I have begun negotiations with the bank. I am feeling strong and confident.

Andy

¶

Dear Anita,

Yesterday I picked up from the sidewalk a small brown bird that had tumbled from its nest—wide clown mouth and stubby wings like tiny flippers. As I cupped it in my hand, I thought of the heedless cruelty of nature and the plight of all those driven untimely from the nest, who must strive against the pangs of loneliness even as they search for food. Like the little bird, I felt at that moment helpless and naked in the face of a world whose haphazardness is difficult to comprehend; and then, thoughts being what they are, uncontrollable and yet connected, I thought of you and of our two days in Rochester. Was it only two? No. It was an eternity, an instant, or both. As I wrote in a poem once: "How we do writhe to the tricks of time." (Or maybe it was "in the clinch of time." I forget.) With such thoughts in mind, I have rushed home to pen this letter.

Seated at my desk I gaze out the window to where a mighty elm once stood that stands no more. It was but yesterday, as the saying goes. Like us, like our "affair," it was sawed off at the knees. I stare out, pensive, and let the reel of time unspool, while I relive in memory frame by frame our two days of passion in that rumpled nest of damp sheets and pillows. Two fabulous days . . . and then? And then I went back to mine, and you to yours. But *why*?

I wonder, Anita, whether like me you sometimes ask yourself that. Was it really just a feeling of obligation toward those others to whom we had once made a careless promise? I know we wanted to believe it was that. I remember how, waiting at the airport for the departure of our separate planes, we spoke of "poor Jolie" and "poor Rick" and we felt self-sacrificing and noble and sorry for ourselves. Our lips touched for the last time, momentarily and roughly, for we were standing in the boarding gate and people were shoving and pushing to get past. Crossing the tarmac to my plane I glanced back and saw a row of faces looking out from the terminal, noses and lips grotesquely flattened against the glass. Which one was yours? I didn't know, so I blew kisses to them all.

How different it all looks in retrospect. Now I see not much nobility and a good deal of cowardice. We turned aside from a torrent that, had we launched our frail craft upon it, might have carried us who knows where—into a whirlpool perhaps, or, equally perhaps, to a small island with a coconut tree! We chose instead to continue paddling in the quiet pools of domesticity, though we knew in our hearts that those pools were already congealing to stagnant fens! I discovered that soon enough in the crudest and most painful manner, and I have just received news through Stephanie M. that you fared no better. We thought of *them*, but did they ever think of *us*? If it is any comfort to you, let me say that I have always considered Rick to be a perfect asshole, as does everyone else who knows him.

Anita, so much water has passed under so many bridges that I fear we've let happiness slip from our grasp. Eight turbulent years, and the image of you in my mind is as untarnished as if minted yesterday. I can still see you as you were on our last night together, seated on the edge of the bed in that dingy cement-block motel on the outskirts of Rochester. A huge neon sign flashing just outside the window is casting the room in alternating tints of garish green and red. Your head is lowered, your breasts bare, your damp hair falls in a dark curtain across your face. In the changing half-light you are looking down at a large menu lying open on your knees. Now the camera zooms out, and I am in the picture as well. I am leaning against a dresser, my elbow resting on a stack of empty pizza boxes. I am wearing just my trousers, a pair of charcoal J.C. Penney slacks, without shirt or socks. The carpet at my feet is littered with cast-off clothes and Budweiser cans. It is, as they say, the end of an affair. We are trying to decide whether to order meatballs or pepperoni. Concealed from your gaze by that curtain of hair, I am staring intently at you, attempting to fix this image in my mind, while you prattle on about toppings. I succeeded only too well, it seems, for the image is still there today, indelible and tormenting: salient against the dark of your summer tan, your breasts are turning green and red, semaphores flashing in the dark night of memory.

Is it really too late, Anita? I realize you may already have found happiness in some new relationship—the news I have of you is tardy and stale—or perhaps you are immersed in your work and too busy to spare an idle thought for an old flame, if that is what I am. Tear up this letter then, toss it into the wastebasket with the Kleenex and candy wrappers. Or don't. Listen to your heart. I *had* to write. I told myself that it's never wrong to clasp at straws, and having clasped, swim on. Whatever happens, upon what strange shore I am finally tossed, I'll be glad that I have written. It is as if the little bird I held in my hand had spread its small wings and flown, even though it was dead.

Affectionately,

Andrew

¶

What is it about me that makes me want to make a fool of myself? I suppose at bottom it's just a perverse form of vanity, the cut-up in class who makes himself into an idiotic spectacle in order not to vanish altogether. But still, I am not pretending, and the mortification I feel in these situations is perfectly genuine. I write a letter, blushing with shame at every sentence, right to the tips of my ears, and send it off; and walking back to the house from the mailbox I catch myself muttering, "That'll show 'em."

¶

Dear Captain Barrows,

I share your dismay at the state of American writing. It is quite true that everywhere one looks one sees cynicism and mockery and that we have lost sight of the great humanist tradition, whatever that was. In addition, as you say, most people use shoddy grammar, which does not reflect well on their parents and teachers, whoever they were. I am, however, not personally able to do anything about this.

Sincerely,

Andrew Whittaker

¶

Dear Mr. Kohlblink,

As I have said twice before, all submissions must be typed.

¶

Dear Jolie,

I wrote just a few days ago, I think it was, and already there are new things to say. I have been trying to play things down in my letters, to wear a brave face, as they say, over the other one, the ghastly drawn one that leers at me in the bathroom every morning, but you may have divined that I have been fairly pushed to the wall lately, backed into a corner. People would like me just to roll over and play dead, or maybe even *be* dead in the case of some of them. I feel exposed, hedged about, and vulnerable. Yet at the same time I am bristling with confidence. I am not going to take this lying down. I am taking steps. The first will be to establish a draconian regime of perfect parsimony when it comes to personal expenditures. With that in view I have had all phone service discontinued. If you've been trying unsuccessfully to call, that's the reason. The next step will be to move out of here and into that little Polk Street efficiency, which no one seems to want anyway, while putting this place up for rent. To do that, to go from an eight-room house to a one-room flat, I am going to have to jettison a mountain of stuff, a lot of it yours. So if there are things here you're still attached to, you need to send me the list right away. The instant I said to myself, Andy, you need to move out of this house, I felt a huge weight lift from me. The expression has it that the burden is on the shoulders, but lately I've been feeling it more as a tremendous pressure in my head. I'm using a toothpick

37

to hold my cigarettes so I can smoke them right down to my lips. I figure this will mean four fewer cigarettes in a day, saving a pack every five days, six packs a month, and so on. Same thing with carrots. I mean, you don't have to cut that little green bit off the end.

Digging through the stuff in the basement, I've run into a lot of spiders, as you can well imagine. I have carried a wooden spoon down from the kitchen, and I use it to push the webs out of the way. I endeavor to do this without hurting the spiders, and usually they scuttle off unharmed, but sometimes things go wrong. If only they were not so soft-bodied and vulnerable. It would be easier to swat them if they had some sort of shell. When a spider dies, it curls up, draws its legs under it, and shrivels. It seems actually to grow smaller, as if the air had gone out of it. That's why I don't want to kill them, because I hate to watch them do that. And yet they often possess a painful bite, and if you see them magnified you'll notice their horrible faces.

Also in the basement, interlaced with the spiders, is all the stuff we moved out of Mama's house. I can't understand why we thought she was likely to *ever* want any of it. They accumulate all this stuff, treasures and mementos and so-called useful items, and the next generation comes along and sees that it's just a pile of rubbish. Looking at it strewn across the basement floor, I couldn't help thinking about the passage of time and the paths of glory leading to the grave, etc. Standing there, holding the spoon in one hand and Mama's college annual in the other, the word "detritus" rang in my head like a bell, tolled like a funeral knell, as they used to say, used to be able to say without cracking up. I'm sorry to run on like this, but it's been raining steadily here for three days.

Among Mama's things, I found a silver and ivory brooch, which might be worth something, and my immediate thought was, I have to show this to Jolie. I miss having you around to talk to. I even miss the way you used to press your hands against your ears when you thought I was holding forth too long. It's odd how the most irritating traits of the people we love can come to seem endearing when they are gone, when they, the people, are gone. I think also of Papa's habit of sticking little bits of toilet paper on the bathroom mirror, I never knew why, or yours of blinking rapidly when I would try to explain something to you.

I spent two days carrying up all the junk and debris, brought it all up and stacked it in the dining room, which I never use anyway: the lawn mower, thick with a sticky melange of oil and dirt, four kinds of shovels (for snow, dirt, ashes, and, I suppose, flower bulbs), all of them rusted, two car batteries, tufts of blue moss sprouting from the terminals, two ladders, one with three broken rungs (what use did we think we would ever have for that?), several broken chairs, Papa's enormous old Philco radio, minus all the knobs, axe, pickaxe, hoe, snow tires (flat), storm windows (two of them cracked), a duffel bag stuffed full with Papa's old leather shoes (stiff as boards), a large expensive painter's easel (remember that?), a shoebox bristling with Mama's plastic hair curlers like a nest of little pink hedgehogs, a box of her stained flesh-colored girdles (the horror!), a dozen brass curtain rods (for what windows? in whose house?), your bicycle, a black ceramic umbrella stand, an American flag. I had almost finished, was tugging a roll of fiberglass batting out from where it was wedged beneath the basement steps, when I spotted the scaly thing: it looked like a dusty carp. The thing was so coated with dust it took me a moment of bug-eyed staring to recognize that it was one of Sokal's snakeskin boots. I found the other one too, farther back under the stairs. And all this stuff is just a minute piece of the whole. A person can't get sideways into the dining room anymore. I had to shove the last pieces in there with main force and pile the overflow in the hall. Which will prove convenient when the time comes to toss it all: just open the front door and *heave*. If it ever stops raining.

The tenants at the duplex, which I finally managed to rent just two weeks ago, went to the city about the roof, so I had to send a roofer over there. He says it's not just the shingles; the sheathing underneath is rotten. He absolutely refuses to start work unless I pay in advance, and now the city has made me take the whole thing, even the half that doesn't leak, off the market until it's fixed.

Love,

Andy

¶

The man stared at the girl as if puzzled by some memory. He then turned on his heels and disappeared inside the shack, for that is what it was. The girl, whose name was Florence, gazed after him a long time. She noticed the grass in the yard needed cutting, and she kept this in mind as she pedaled off, for it was nearly supper time and she had to buy eggs. Though her family were small farmers, they did not have chickens. Or they had chickens, but they had been struck down by a blight. The remaining flock, for most had died, wandered about the farmyard in a daze, clucking mournfully. It was a desolate scene, and contemplating it from the porch, where he sat in an old wooden rocker, had caused her father to wear an expression of great sadness which he was able to banish only in the presence of his daughter, who would read to him from the Almanac. She had little time for this lately, as she had to do the milking as well as the plowing and reaping, not to mention nursing the sick chickens. Her father had been in a wheelchair ever since he was struck by a hit-and-run driver while crossing the highway to get the mail, which included his beloved Almanac, strewn on the pavement beside him. His sun-burnished visage was still rugged, though bristled, for he often did not shave. And before she reaped, she sowed. Wheat and barley and other grains, probably. Meanwhile, the man sat on a bed, on a bare mattress with the springs poking out and stains from generations of strangers, and tried to think of nothing, for that is what he had come to, what he had come to this desolate place for. It was his beloved childhood home from before his parents had let their desire for modern appliances tear the family away. They had been small farmers. They were Amish probably, and they did not associate with the family on the grand farm up the road from whence Florence had ridden on her bicycle that significant morning. There had been bad feelings between the two families for over eighty years, though neither Florence nor the man, whose name was Adrian, or Adam, was aware of this. But Florence's father was—he was a hard, bitter, hard-bitten man— as was Adam's mother, who though once beautiful was now a half-forgotten figure in a nursing home in Burbank, California, a strand of gray hair falling across her still youthful features. As a girl she had been known far and wide for her fiery temper and unkempt hair, and this had frightened most suitors away, though not the randy young hellion who would become

41

Adam's father. He was not a man to walk behind a plow or to cut ice from the lake in winter using a large hand saw. Packed under straw in the cellar the ice melted very slowly, but still by July they were drinking warm sodas, if they could afford them, and warm unpurified branch water otherwise. Until one blazing August day, when Adam's father staggered in from the fields. His young wife, her face flushed and beaded with sweat, handed him a glass of hot Coke, as she was wont to do. He took a big swig, and his whole body revolted. A spray of sweet brown liquid fell on the stack of clean dry clothes his wife had just taken in from the line after washing them in the little stream back of the house. "Pack the bags," he muttered, wiping his chin with his hand. So he had taken his wife and infant son off to southern California, and to Adam growing up the old farm had been only a black-and-white photograph on the wall of a pleasant living room in Glendale, where the picture window framed a pomegranate tree. And now in this strange yet familiar land, which would be snow-bound one day and where "pomegranate" was only a word in a dictionary, sitting on the soiled mattress, he tried to think of nothing as he had vowed he would do. Yet the figure of the raven-haired girl on the bicycle impinged upon his wounded psyche like a moth battering its wings against the light of a dying bulb.

¶

Dear Marvin,

Much as I would like to make amends for the screwup, I really can't reprint your poems in the next issue. They were legible, with a little effort, in at least half the copies, and the people who got those copies, and who worked at making them out the first time, certainly don't want to open the next issue and find them in there again. Send me something else, and if it's any good, I'll print that.

All the best,
Andrew

¶

Dear Miss Moss,

Rest assured, when I suggested you send your poems to *American Pony* I did not mean it as a "put-down." I thought, and still think, that would be a good place for you to start. It does not mean that I think you write "dumb poems." I have said already what I think of your writing; and if I said it, I meant it. I am not in the business of being polite. I am sorry to hear that your parents are so unsympathetic to your aspirations—I suffered similar misunderstandings when I was young, especially from my father, who raised dogs and thought I should become a veterinarian, but nothing quite on the scale you describe, and of course it's easier for a boy. You are lucky to have the support of someone like Mr. Caldwell—perhaps he can do something. As for me, I really can't offer advice as to whether you should "cut out," and I don't know anywhere in San Francisco you could stay. Please understand, this is all quite beyond me. As for your wish to send me more of your writing, even if not for publication, I can scarcely say no, under the circumstances. However, you must keep in mind that I am a busy person, even a harried person, and right now I am caught up in all sorts of very disagreeable financial entanglements, plus I am in the process of moving from my present house, forced out, really, by an accumulation of stuff, so I can't promise more than a few quick notes in the margins, just whatever comes to mind as I read on the fly. And please do enclose a stamped return envelope.

    Sincerely,

    Andrew Whittaker

¶

Dear Jolie,

    It is three a.m. I fell asleep early but then woke up at midnight and have been awake since. I am not even tired. I seem to be able to get by with very little sleep lately. I thought about going for a walk but am afraid it will rain again, so I am going to tell you about something I discovered in the basement. Do you remember the stack of photo albums we carted over from Mama's place? It wouldn't surprise me that you don't. We were so harried by work at the time, and so caught up in our quarrels, and so angry, really, at Mama for the way she was behaving, that we scarcely did more than leaf through a few pages before stowing them in the basement with the rest of her trash. I had forgotten all about them myself. But last week found me sitting on one of those blue plastic milk boxes, my back propped against the warm metal of the faintly vibrating clothes dryer, with the albums spread open on the floor at my feet. The rhythmic clicking of the dryer—I had washed my plaid shirt, the one with the zipper—mingled with the susurration of the rain and the odor of mold in the basement to create the perfect ambience for a journey into the past. I went through the albums page by page. What struck me first was that Mama had glued the photos in there without regard to order. A photo of Papa at fifty would be followed by one of Peg at two. She used to keep all of them in a cardboard box at the back of her bedroom closet, and every Christmas Eve she would drag it out and dump the pictures in a heap on the living-room rug, where we would sit and dig through them and sometimes fight over them. That was a long time ago. I suppose when she got the albums—it must have been after she started saving greenback stamps, at the same time as she "earned" (as she liked to put it) the set of cheapo aluminum pans she gave us—she just stuck the pictures in higgledy-piggledy as they came to hand.

I suppose this randomness is what caused us when we were leafing through the albums back then to miss the odd thing I am going to tell you. I could not be certain of it myself until I had removed all the photos from the albums and laid them out on the floor, even though that meant badly ripping a fair number.

You remember how I used to complain that I had practically no memories of childhood, at least nothing comparable to the stuff other people seem able to dredge up at the drop of a handkerchief? You, for example, are able to prattle for hours about things as trivial as the ruffled dress you wore to a little friend's birthday party when you were six and she was seven, while I possess, as testimony to my existence in the past, nothing but a few dull or squalid images stuck in my head like snapshots, static and without relation to anything before or after, undated and therefore almost without meaning. In college, when people would sit around swapping memories, I was forced to make things up.

Some of the photos have notations on the back, e.g., "Peg and Papa at Deer Lake," "Andy and Peg eating watermelon," but those rarely include a date. So once I had cleared a space in the living room and could finally apply myself to putting the pictures in temporal order I had to rely almost entirely on evidence furnished by the pictures themselves: the gradually increasing size of both Peg and myself, the steady puckering and sallowing of my parents' skin, the ineluctable swelling of their waistlines, the appearance and then disappearance of several cats and dogs, the gradual thinning of Papa's hair and the increasingly ineffectual combings with which he attempted to hide it, and of course the progression in the model years of the automobiles against which we were posed with depressing regularity. It took me two days of arrangement and rearrangement—in the course of which I several times had to shift hundreds of photos a fraction of a centimeter one way or another on the floor in order to open a space farther down the line big enough to insert a single new one—before I at last had them all laid out in a vast spiral with me in a lacy bassinet at the center and me again at the end, this time a sullen and shirtless teenager seated on the front steps of our house on Laurel Avenue, a menacing scowl just visible behind two upright middle fingers.

There are pictures of me when I was small—alone or with Peg or with animals, at parties and at Christmas—up to perhaps the third grade. These pictures show a solemn, unsmiling child, serious and yet—one senses this—probably not sad. His hair is blond, or at least it's not brown. Then there are pictures of me as an acne-pocked teenager, hair several shades darker (due perhaps to the over-ample application of Vitalis or Brylcreem suggested by its unnatural gleam) with pants pulled very high and cinched tightly by a narrow belt. I wanted to write "cinched painfully tight," but since I can't actually remember how it felt that would have been only a guess. Mismatched argyle socks are clearly visible at the base of the hitched pants, and I am wearing heavy brown shoes at a epoch when other boys were wearing penny loafers. And there is a shot of me in a baggy bathing suit at some lake, my skinny legs looking like bamboo shoots in oversized flowerpots, but of course upside down—the flowerpots, I mean, would have to be upside down. And of course I have grown larger, though at first glance my head appears not to have kept pace. In these later photos, without exception, I appear sullen and resentful. Perhaps that was how I was. Or perhaps I appear that way only because I didn't like having my picture taken. In fact, knowing my picture was about to be taken must have made me think with shame of my appearance, as it probably would still if I could feel that it was *my* appearance, if I could manage to greet the person in those pictures as someone other than a stranger, if, in other words, I could *remember* him. I look at the pictures, and I say to myself, *Yes, that's me*, but I don't feel the warmth of recognition.

Between these two groups of photographs intervenes, I estimate, a gap of some seven or eight years. I retain only the meagerest handful of recollections from that epoch, and now, with all the snapshots laid out on the floor, I have discovered *there are no photographs either!* Why, during all this long interval, so important in the life of a child, did no one bother to take my picture? There are innumerable shots of Peg from the same period: Peg at the beach, Peg on her pony. By all rights I should be there with her in some of them. In fact, in a number of the pictures she appears to be standing at the side of the frame, as if she were leaving room for me. It's as though I had vanished, a cute kid, or at any rate, a normal one, who disappears for a long while, only to reappear as a grossly unattractive, larger individual. I would write Peg about this except I know she would never answer.

It was only tonight, while I was lying in bed not able to sleep, that it dawned upon me that not only are so many of my memories *like* snapshots, in their isolation and immobility, they are *of* snapshots, of these *same* snapshots, which as an adult I must have seen numerous times at Mama's house, every Christmas in fact. Apart from them, I have next to nothing.

Your card arrived this afternoon. I had hoped you would be more understanding about the money. Two months is not going to cut it, though it will help. It's just possible, assuming I can rent this place and two others that are vacant, that I will be in a position to send you something more next month. But the fact is they are in terrible shape and I don't have the money to fix them. I know New York is expensive, but no one asked you to move there. As for me, I drive all the way across town to the new Safeway, robbing valuable hours from other things, just to save a few pennies. You might, as you hop into your next taxi to Manhattan, think of that.

Love,

Andrew

¶

potatoes (lots)
cans (chili, soups, Big John's Beans)
liverwurst
marg
hocks
puffs
cupcakes
maybe steak or meat
p. chop
shoe polish
tuna
sardines
cheese snack
froz fries—coupons
lunch stuff
bread
cereal
t.p. (lots)
miracle whip
lightbulbs
money order
½" shut-off valve
vodka
earplugs

¶

Dear Harold,

Of course I remember you. I think it interesting that you
have gone into agriculture. I myself feel very close to the land
even when I am exiled in the city, as I must be, because of its

advantages to someone who must always be before the public, in its eye, as they say, or up its ass, as I sometimes am. As for machinery, etc., I couldn't judge. So you *did* marry Catherine in the end. How we did vie for her! May the best man win, as they say, and I am sure he did. Jolie and I separated two years ago. I have kept the house, a Victorian box much too large for me, which I am finding impossible to keep remotely tidy. I spend several hours cleaning, and a few days later it's back where it was. It's quite a lonely house sometimes and I've thought of getting a dog, but I'm afraid of getting a biter. I have an office in the house, where I do my writing and editing, so I don't have to go out very often. I imagine one of the great things about living in the country is not having neighbors. Of course if you are in this area you must stop by, though I don't think I could "tie one on" with you. I have some small health problems. Nothing serious but I have to be a wee bit careful. And the people in the bars have grown so terribly young. I imagine that you, working outside in all kinds of weather, are just bursting with good health, and you probably look younger than you are. I have a funny noise in my chest sometimes. We make choices so early, and on the basis of practically no information, and then we end up with these different lives that we are really stuck with. It's all so depressing. We get ourselves boxed in and then there seems no way out. I think if I did more exercise I would feel better, but I don't want to start anything too strenuous, you know, because of the noise. I am basically a desk worker. Very boring. Be sure to let me know if you are passing, as I don't like surprises. What kind of things do you grow?

Andy

AUGUST

Dear Mama,

I've been going through your old photo albums, looking for a few nice pictures for your room. How funny those old bathing suits seem now, though you were quite a dish! My memories of Papa are of a shortish, fat man with a cigar, and it's strange to see him looking so trim, and with that little mustache, like the bad guy in an old movie. Glancing over the photos, I couldn't help noticing that there are hardly any pictures of me between the ages of about seven and fifteen, and that has set me to wondering. You used to tell me how disappointed Papa was in me when I was a child, at a time when the sons of all his friends were excelling. Actually I think the word you used was "embarrassed." Could that have led him—out of grief, perhaps—to not want to have any pictures of me around the house? I can imagine he might experience them as an unpleasant doubling. I mean there I was and there I would be again on the mantel or someplace. Or he might have worried that the photographs would later become painful reminders. If this seems unlikely to you, as it does to me, maybe you have some other explanation, in which case I would be happy to hear it. Perhaps you could drop me a line as I'm not going to be able to run up next month as planned.

Your loving son,

Andy

p.s. to Mrs. Robinson:

I know, if Mama is getting this letter, it is because you are reading it to her, for which I say thanks a million. I know how forgetful she is and how spiteful sometimes, especially when she feels she is being criticized. I am not blaming her for not taking any pictures of me for all those years. I don't care about pictures; I am just wondering why there aren't any. I mean, most mothers *enjoy* taking pictures. I hope that despite your understandable difficulties with Mama, or perhaps even because of them, you will consent to help me out on this matter. You will need to find some way of getting Mama off her guard. For example, you could chat about your own children, if you have any, or you could just make some up, if you don't, and then you could remark how hard it is to take good pictures of children, they being so rambunctious. At that point Mama might chime in with some information of her own. For example, she might say that it's easier to take pictures of girls, and that would be an important clue. I leave the details to your good judgment. I would be very grateful if you would drop me a line about anything you might learn. I think it only fair that you accept the ten-dollar bill you will find taped inside the envelope. I didn't want it to fall out in front of Mama, as she would naturally assume it was for her.

Sincerely,

Andy Whittaker

¶

Dear Contributor,

Thank you for giving us the opportunity to read your work. After careful consideration, we have reluctantly concluded that it does not meet our needs at this time.

The Editors at *Soap*

¶

Dear Miss Moss,

Thank you for the chocolates, the pictures, and the wallet. Did you make that yourself? Also, of course, the new poems and the envelope. I'll get to the poems just as soon as I can find a spare hour, when I can give them my full attention. I am touched that you thought of sending me this package in the midst of everything. And I do appreciate your words of concern at my situation. However, the financial entanglements I mentioned really have nothing at all to do with embezzlement or things of that sort, just a little accounting mix-up. And the fact that I am being forced to move does not mean that I am "on the run." Sorry to disappoint. I'm afraid you'll have to look elsewhere for your "shady dealer." I am, I regret, not nearly that interesting.

And sorry again, but I really can't give you *any* advice about your situation at home. Furthermore, since you don't tell me what was in the diary, you cannot expect me to pass judgment on the behavior of your parents. I will say that as a general rule I think people ought not to read other people's private papers. But that said, the fact that you left the diary open on the coffee table suggests to me that you were, to put it bluntly, spoiling for a fight. As for God, I am not simply an agnostic—I am an indifferentist. The ministers, pastors, and padres I have met have generally been fools or charlatans. I surmise from your description Rev. Hanley is both. I admire your ability to make a funny story out of what must have been a really painful interview. You must keep in mind that it's a big world beyond Rufus. You should also keep in mind that it will still be there next year, probably.

Thank you for the pictures. They were quite a surprise. I had rather expected, I don't know why, a dumpy creature with pimples and large black shoes, not an attractive young woman in tennis shorts. It's no wonder the good pastor had his hands all over you. I hope you won't think that an insensitive remark, and I am not trying to excuse him, but I believe in acknowledging what's in front of me.

Sincerely,

Andy Whittaker

¶

Dear Dahlberg,

I turned down your last submission due to its lack of merit, and the fact that you are Canadian had nothing to do with it, but if it makes you feel better to believe that, then go ahead.

With regards.

Andy

¶

Dear Peg,

I know you don't like hearing from me or Mama, but I have to ask you a question. I really wouldn't if it only concerned me, but other people are involved. *Home and Ranch Magazine* is planning to run a longish profile of me called "The Making of a Writing Man," and they want photographs from my childhood. They want one of you as well, perhaps even several. I have looked through all Mama's photos and there is not a single picture of me between the ages of about seven and fourteen, and I have been wondering why. There are many of you and Papa and Mama and even the animals. But of course the magazine won't run any of those, attractive as they are, if I can't produce at least two or three of me. Obviously someone has gone through the photo albums and systematically removed my pictures. I know that sounds fantastic, and whoever did it was quite careful and patient, moving around the other photos to fill the blank places. I am not making any accusations, though I can't imagine who else might have done it. I'm talking about opportunity and motive. If you did take them, perhaps accidentally, and did not utterly destroy them by shredding or flushing, perhaps you could return a handful.

Your brother,
Andy

¶

ATTENTION ALL TENANTS

IF YOU HAVE MISLPACED YOUR MAILBOX KEY, CONTACT PHELPS IN 1A. SHE HAS A MASTER KEY AND WILL RETRIEVE YOUR MAIL. DO NOT TRY TO PRY THE BOXES OPEN!

¶

Dear Mr. Fontini,

I have received your message. I have given it careful consideration. I can assure you it is not plausible to blame the plumbing. There is nothing wrong with the plumbing. Not only did Sewell find nothing wrong, but I personally went over every inch of it after the first incident. I went over it with ruler and calipers. The tub's overflow pipe is of the standard size. If you don't trust me or Sewell (who is after all a licensed plumber), you are welcome to call the city inspector, assuming you can get him to come, which I doubt once he hears both sides of the story. "If not faulty plumbing," you will say, "then why has the ceiling fallen on my supper, not once but twice?" The explanation, I believe, lies close at hand, indeed, one could say it is even closer than that. I think you would do well to look attentively at your wife while she bathes. If you do this, I think you will observe the following sequence.

(1) Mrs. Fontini turns on the taps and lets the tub fill while she removes her garments, looks for the shampoo, perhaps not finding it right away, goes to the linen closet for a clean towel, etc.

(2) While she is thus occupied, the water in the bathtub is busy rising to the level of the overflow pipe, the excess gurgling down it, which doesn't bother her, as she knows there is a large electric water heater in the basement.

(3) Getting into the tub, she overlooks her own not-inconsiderable bulk as well as Archimedes' experience in the bath, where he discovered that for every cubic inch of Mrs. Fontini submerged in bath water a corresponding cubic inch of said water will rise toward the rim of the tub.

(4) She either never knew or has forgotten that the overflow pipe is designed to handle only the gradual rise in water occasioned by an open faucet and was never intended to cope with sudden surges. Perhaps her arms, though large and braced firmly against the sides of the tub, are simply not up to the task of effectuating the gradual lowering of the rest of her bulk into the water, and as a consequence she just lets herself plop.

The cumulative effect of steps (1) through (4) is a tidal surge that overtops the tub's meager levees and spills bucket-size dollops of warm bath water onto the bathroom floor. From there it makes its way under the influence of gravity down between the tiles and onto the sheetrock of the kitchen ceiling. At which point its descent is not stopped but merely slowed, while the sheetrock gradually softens until it is finally soft enough to tumble precipitously onto your supper. I don't want to be the cause of discord between husband and wife, but unless you would like to be billed for the regular replacement of the kitchen ceiling I suggest that Mrs. Fontini convert to showering, or, if she really must have baths and is unable or unwilling to lower herself into the water at a normal pace, that you devise some sort of lowering mechanism for her, perhaps a tackle using ropes and pulleys. With this I wish you every success, but please do not use nails in the walls. In the meantime, you must remit to the Whittaker Company $317 for repairs to the ceiling.

Sincerely,
The landlord

¶

What does it mean that I have such a gift for writing unpleasant letters? Does it say something about my character, that maybe I am not a nice person? Or maybe it just means that other people are not nice persons. I once struggled to write simple thank-you notes when people sent me presents; the notes always sounded totally insincere. It never helped at all that I sometimes actually liked the presents. It was the same when I used to tell Jolie that I loved her. I could hear myself sounding like the worst kind of ham and liar, even though I really did love her. I suppose this was part of the reason I was so horrid to her later. Now I write people whom I barely know, and the letters positively sparkle, especially when they give me an opportunity to be unpleasant in a snide way to people who can't do anything about it. Maybe Baudelaire was right, and the spleen really is the creative organ.

¶

Dear Mrs. Lipsocket,

You have been sending me your poems off and on for four years. For the first three of those I labored to comment, comforting you with platitudes, while covertly advising you tactfully to chuck it. Yet you have continued against all odds. You have written me pitiful letters. You have wrung my heart with descriptions of your literary sufferings, with which I have sympathized; your outsized ambitions, which are so like my own; your ovarian problems, the cruelty of your library committee, and your husband's philandering, which I have felt incompetent to address. You have been the cause of a broken sleep in which I dream that I am beating small animals. Faced with this, I surrender. I have not kept copies of your past efforts, and your present work seems worse than ever, so I leave it up to you: choose any six lines, and I will print them. After that I am not going to open any envelopes from you.

Sincerely,

Andy Whittaker

¶

Kind Sirs,

I read in the paper about Fellowship Christian Tabernacle's program "Neighbors Helping Neighbors." I was moved by your efforts and the huge amount of money you have raised—all those bake sales, raffles, and car washes. I was particularly impressed by the two-and-a-half tons of aluminum cans. I am not a member of your church, or any church, but I gather from the article that you still consider me to be your neighbor. I am appreciative of that sentiment, and if ever I do go to church—which I may in the future—it will certainly be at your establishment. I am a widower living alone. I am not old, but my health is far from perfect. I have a noise in my chest. I am finding the care and cleaning of my house increasingly taxing and difficult, especially getting the dust bunnies out, which I now see are everywhere under things, especially beds and sofas. I find that when I bend over the noise gets worse, and my breath makes them scoot away and become harder to catch. The house is old and full of china knickknacks—treasures of my late wife—that have to be picked up and dusted and put back, which takes hours and is difficult for someone whose hands have a tendency to shake. I would be broken-hearted if I dropped one. I know I would hear Claudine reproach me, as she was ever wont to do, and I couldn't bear that now. I have everything needed except a squeegee to wash the windows. My wife always used balled-up newspaper and vinegar, which I never thought was a good idea, since it left black streaks, although she denied this. My phone service has become unreliable due to work they are doing in the street. I am home almost all the time, so if you think that I am a "worthy cause" you could just send someone over.

Your neighbor,
Andrew Whittaker.

¶

Dear Harold,

Thanks for your letter; it was so very friendly. I too would like to have a regular correspondence. You must have read between the lines of my letter that I am really not well. It's not just the chest; I am finding the house in which I am now living to be very oppressive, especially when it rains, as it has been doing practically nonstop for days, especially when it is untidy and cluttered, as it inevitably is, for reasons I can't get to the bottom of, since I seem to be always cleaning. It's not the rain itself so much as the silence the rain brings with it, the way the sound of the rain on the roof and windows makes the quiet inside the house so much more noticeable, perhaps because it drowns out the little noises I otherwise make, the padding of bare feet on the floor, the scratching of a pen, an occasional gentle clearing of the throat. I think of you and your work outdoors with plants and animals, and I am horribly envious. I lie on my back on the floor, looking up at the ceiling for leaks, and I think of you bouncing across the furrows on a tractor. I suppose it is often sunny down there. I have been working on a new story, set in the Wisconsin farm country (where I have never actually been), and it would be great if you could answer some technical questions now and then. Maybe I could even come down for a short visit, get a feeling for farm life. Your family sounds wonderful, and I am very fond of animals, especially baby donkeys.

I have decided to move out of my house into a smaller place, where there will be less room for ghosts, and I have been packing things into boxes. I have a regular wall of boxes stacked in the living room. I can scarcely see out the front windows anymore. In the evening, when the light through the rain-streaked panes has softened the edges of the boxes, they look like sandbags, and I have the comfortable feeling of being fortified. I have closed off the dining room, since it's jam full of stuff I brought up from the basement, and the hall is almost full as well. There is a hemmed-in feeling to the house now. Fortified, or hemmed in—it's difficult to know what one feels nowadays. Packing the books has been particularly slow, because I keep finding ones I had forgotten I owned, and I end up sitting on the floor reading, my quiet breath and the occasional scrape of a turning page drowned, as I mentioned, by the constant susurration of the rain.

Among those forgotten books, I discovered a huge encyclopedia of mammals, which Jolie must have bought years ago when she imagined she could write stories for children with animals in them, with animals in the stories. Or perhaps it descends from my father, who was fond of animals, especially dogs. My mother, who is still alive, says he had always wanted me to become a veterinarian and was disappointed when I decided to major in English, though I don't remember him ever saying anything about that to me. Right now, the life of a busy veterinarian strikes me as quite interesting and desirable, as something I might have striven for had it occurred to me.

I must never have looked at the book before. You can't imagine how many animals there are that almost no one has ever heard of—sportive lemurs, needle-clawed bush babies, warty pigs, oriental spiny rats, punctated grass-mice, golden-rumped elephant shrews, and fairy armadillos, to pick a few at random. Such fabulous names—it's obvious that among those creeping around in the jungle in pith helmets were at least a few mad poets. And what do you know about the ai?

Next to nothing, I imagine. So you'll be surprised to learn, as I just have, that it is a variety of three-toed sloth, even though it has, in fact, three fingers. For some reason the early naturalists were quite confused when it came to fingers and toes. This seems to me odd; are you ever confused about them? I wonder if it had anything to do with the fact that they wore gloves, the naturalists, I mean, in those days often wore gloves. All sloths have three toes. As for fingers, some have two and some have three. The ai (*Bradypus torquatus*) has three of each, that is, six at each end of it, evenly divided. It moves so slowly and hangs out (literally) in such damp leafy places that green algae grows on its fur. As has happened to me during the current monsoon, or so it seems. There is mildew on everything, and I myself am feeling quite mossy in spots. As for inactivity, I don't think I've moved two hundred yards in the past two days. Where would I move to, with the rain coming down as if for Noah's flood? The sloth is, I suppose, the only green mammal. That's odd when you think about it, considering how many green creatures there are otherwise, grasshoppers and frogs, for example. The green coloration is thought to help it hide from predators; from jaguars, I suppose, who must mistake it for a pile of leaves. The resourceful animal is, furthermore, alleged to breed colonies of "cockroach-like moths" in its green fur, though to what useful purpose the book doesn't let on. Nor do I get a clear picture of those little creatures—I can't imagine a less cockroach-like insect than a moth. I have not personally, even during the worst of my pluvial solitude, bred any of those, though I did a few nights ago find something awful crawling inside my pajama shirt. I had turned off the light and had just lain down on the bed. I always begin the night on my back, because it's a yogic principle, and also lately because of the noise in my chest, which seems to become less intense in that position, or maybe just less audible, due to the soft pillow folding up around my ears. Though the creature must have been in there ever since my shower an hour earlier, it only began moving about when it found itself being crushed between my back and the mattress. It possessed, as I could tell from the texture of its walk, little spines along the backs of its legs. It was like being stabbed with rows of needles. I of course sprang up and tore off the shirt, pulling it violently off over my head. In the process I inadvertently flung the creature across the room—it struck the wall with a loud *tick*. It was quite dead when I found it in the morning; a large black beetle.

During the past several months I have moved my bowels once every day with clockwork regularity. I mention this because the ai shits and pisses only once a week—a remarkable achievement for what seems otherwise a rather stupid animal. It does it at the base of its tree. It feeds on leaves and pawpaws. Studying the photos in my book, however, it seems to me its head is too small for its body, and not just because it appears to have no ears. We seem to have here a violation of some sort of universal law of proportions. Curiously, this is something I have thought about myself as well, that my head seems to be less than normal size. Did I never tell you that? I am not the only one to have thought this. At school they called me BB head. My head is, in fact, not exceptionally small, or only slightly smaller than the norm, as I have verified with statistics at my doctor's. Do you remember it as being smaller than the norm? It only looks that way because my neck is unusually large, and in the absence of contrast the

65

head appears smaller. A simple case of optical illusion. Nevertheless, I'm still self-conscious in this regard—the wounds of childhood never really heal, do they? I prefer winter for that reason, as it permits me to hide my neck in two turns of woolen scarf. Did you ever notice this about me?

You are thinking, aren't you, how he does go on? And you are right, for I have not yet disposed of the ai. Perhaps you are not interested. Fortunately for me I can't discern that from here. Poor Harold, you were always such a wonderful listener. In college I made jokes about the "agricultural engineer" I had for a roommate, amusing my friends with tales of your ineptness and bucolic ignorance, and your comical mispronunciations of unusual words. I still smile when I think how you would accent "plethora" and "amorous" on the second syllable. Marcus Quiller and I used to compete to see which of us could maneuver you into saying one of them in conversation. While in fact just being able to sit on my bed at night, and talk, and have you, in your bed, listen, were among the happiest moments of my college years, the only moments in which I felt I could be myself. I am sorry about the jokes now, perhaps because I have a feeling something similar is happening to me.

The ai (pronounced "I") gets its name from the Portuguese in imitation of the whistling sound the baby of the species makes through its nostrils when it fears it has been abandoned by its mother. "Aie," as you might know, is also the sound a French person makes when slightly wounded, equivalent to the English "ow." Isn't it wonderful how even something as natural as a cry of pain requires a listing in the dictionary? I was thinking someone should do a little booklet containing a list of those words from all the languages of the world, An International Dictionary of Pain. I think I'll do that next. Meanwhile, I have been practicing, and I believe I have learned to do a pretty good imitation of the sloth's cry. I place my thumbs firmly against the openings of my nostrils, blocking them completely. I then give a vigorous snort and at the same time fling both thumbs away from the nostrils in a decisive forward motion. The result is a woofling whistle which I imagine is quite close to what a young ai must sound like. I did it at the post office the other day when the clerk told me I had insufficient postage on my package. She was a mousy creature, so you can imagine the effect when I flung my thumbs from my nose in her direction and fired that noise at her. I could hear them all buzzing behind me as I was leaving the building. In the future I'll always use this device when I want to express contempt, though that's probably not what the baby ai does with it. Do your children imitate barnyard animals or is that something only city children do?

I see this letter is much too long. I wonder if you are still reading. Maybe you got fed up halfway through, and all this time I've been talking to nobody. Imagine a man in a room talking about himself, perhaps in a very boring way, while looking down at the floor. And while he goes on with his monologue, which as I said is of interest only to himself, one by one the other people in the room tiptoe away until he is all alone, the last one shutting the door silently behind him. Finally the man looks up and sees what has happened, and of course he is overcome by feelings of ridicule and shame. Maybe this letter is now at the bottom of your wastepaper basket, a tiny trivial voice in the depths of a tin well, rattling on and on. Is your wastepaper basket made of tin? How unbearably sad. If you have come with me this far, I want to say that I appreciate your company, and also your letters, and would like to have more of those, if you feel like writing again.

Andy

¶

Dear Mr. Watts,

I did receive the notice about the trash. I do understand that you cannot gather up any items that are not bagged, binned, or otherwise confined in approved receptacles. And yes, I am aware that this has happened before. I do not, however, feel that this justifies your use of the phrase "repeat offender." Each time it has happened I have gone over there myself and picked it all up. If you drive by now you will find more than a sufficient number of trash cans; three, to be exact, unless one has been stolen already. It is really not my fault that they don't use them.

Sincerely.

Andrew Whittaker

¶

Ahoy, Willy,

I have had no word from you about the April thing. I know it has been less than three weeks since I wrote, but I had assumed you would jump at the chance for that kind of exposure. Maybe your teaching job lets you feel secure enough that you can turn your back on the larger public, and even your old friends, if that's what you are doing. I envy you the luxury of both. I myself have to descend every day into the pit and battle for a living, and I have been cursed with a dogged loyalty to anyone who has ever given me a pat on the head or a shake to my furry paw. After a month of tropical heat, it has been raining here for weeks. The newspaper is full of pictures of flooded farms. I am getting quite moldy. Moldy and morose. Morose and wondering why I am not hearing from Willy. I have at last begun work on the big novel I had been putting off for so long. I have bided my time, I have practiced my craft, I have collected experiences. And now the words are coming out perfect; I excrete them almost without effort. They land on the page and stay there. I envisage an oddly musical structure: a groaning basso profundo of despair broken by burlesque interludes and periodic shrieks of hysteria. I am especially fond of the shrieks—they strike me as just so *typical*. I think by next April I'll have enough to be able to read a chapter or two at the gala. A lot of people around here have got used to thinking that I'll never produce anything, and so that's sure to make a splash.

Along with the novel, which is the really important thing, I have in the works a very funny parody of that bastard Troy Sokal, set in Wisconsin farm country, same place he puts his novels. Until you've tried it you can't imagine how hard it is to write badly well. And I have ideas for a series of prose poems, little existential parables of tedium and despair, set in Africa probably.

I'd like to tell you more about everything, especially about what the last couple of years have been like, but right now my brand-new maid is turning the house upside down around my ears. I requested an experienced cleaning woman and they sent me a Mexican girl who has to ask how to turn on the vacuum. Charmingly shy, but a little too Aztec for my taste. From the neck down, though, she's what people used to call a tomato.

Let me hear from you soon, as I'll have to invite someone else if you really can't make it.

All the best,

Andy

¶

Dear Peg,

Thank you for your note. I was already aware that I was a great disappointment to Papa and that you were a little princess. You are so disagreeable that I am sorry I ever wrote. Prior to reading your charming note, with its references to my intellectual capacities and my physique, there existed a large number of delightful pictures of you at all stages of childhood, including one on a pony. If you'd like me to send you a box with all the itty-bitty pieces, just let me know.

Your brother,

Andy

¶

The scene: a wide river, sluggish, muddy, some kind of estuary. It is in Africa probably. On both sides of the river, or estuary, a sandy desert stretches away as far as the eye can see. No trees, not even palm trees, dot the landscape. In the beginning, a group of children, boys and girls, dressed in sailor suits and pinafores, are playing, or attempting to play, in the sand. But the sand is extremely fine and dry, almost a dry powder, and they are able to construct only formless piles like anthills. In the face of repeated failures, sweating in their city clothes, the children become quarrelsome and listless, some one and some the other, the quarrelsome ones striking the listless ones sharply in the face or dumping handfuls of hot sand down their shirts, the listless ones lying down in the sand, weeping softly. (They will remember this later.) The grown-ups, meanwhile, men and women whose children these presumably are, also dressed in dark city clothes, the men with top hats and canes, the women with parasols and bustles and exaggerated bosoms, stand in little clusters on the bank, cluster in little stands there, like trees in a landscape without any, and discuss whether the darkish things they see far out in the river are logs, almost submerged after months in the water, or crocodiles. The discussion is tedious, anfractuous, inconclusive. In their heart of hearts, they all, adults and children, would like just to dive in and get it over with.

¶

Dear Anita,

What a terrible misunderstanding. I feel like a complete fool. You can well believe I had no idea you and Rick were back together. But if that's really what you want, what can I do except wish you both all the best? I had meant to write a letter of tender reminiscence about a time that I foolishly thought was important to us both. It hurts me that you say it made you feel pawed. I'll not write again.

Andy

¶

paint thinner
tile mastic
ant poison
garbage can
interior white
I write like my mother
post office
light bill
courthouse
pills
stay home
read
go somewhere
so. comfort
food

¶

Dear Dahlberg,

First you accuse me of rejecting your work out of anti-Canadian prejudice, and now you tell me that thanks to being published in *Soap* you were finally able to get laid. What do you expect me to do with this information?

Andy

¶

GET READY TO BOAST TO YOUR FRIENDS! 125 S. Spalding St. Three-story five-unit traditional style bldng. Two units available. Each unit 2 bdrm 1 bath. Distinctive arched doorways.

Some new wndows. New paint last year. Conveniently located in quiet neighborhood near Interstate. Lighted parking. LIVE FIRST MONTH RENT FREE wth 1 yr lease. $110 + utils.

¶

Dear Jolie,

I have been having some kind of trouble with my eyes. They are bloodshot, and the slightest glare is painful. It seems to me the whites have acquired a yellow cast that makes me look like a drunk.

*

The sun has finally reappeared, having used its two weeks absence to move farther to the south than when we last saw it. With the elm tree gone, there is now nothing to prevent it blazing in through the living room windows for the better part of the day. See above.

*

I don't talk to anyone for days on end. At the grocery store this morning, when I reached the checkout counter and asked the girl for a pack of cigarettes, my voice cracked. I tried to make a joke about it, but she backed away. So I just left.

*

Nixon was on television, performing. With the sound turned off, he might have been anyone.

*

I went around the house with the maid, pointing out what I wanted her to do. I talked constantly, even though she did not understand two words of what I was saying, while she smiled blankly.

*

Someone says, "I know I talk too much, please forgive me," and then goes on and on about that.

*

I am astonished by your suggestion that I "suspend" the magazine for—I think you said—"a couple of years."

*

I have nothing to say, really. Strange, isn't it.

Love,

Andy

¶

Dear Mrs. Brud:

I have your letter. I don't know how long ago you wrote it, as there is no date. When you write in pencil on the back of a flyer advertising gutter repairs and stick it under a person's door, do not expect prompt replies, for it may happen, as it did in fact happen, that the person will take it for an advertising flyer, as in most respects it still is, and if he also is not feeling well and does not like to bend over, because of a noise he hears when he does that, along with a slight breathlessness, he might not pick it up immediately but might instead walk on it for several days before his cleaning woman, who comes for only an hour once a week and who is inexperienced and worried that she might throw away some valuable document, shows it to him while asking "O.K. I toss this?" at which point he looks. I don't care what you told Mr. Brud. I did not try to push you into the bedroom. I was doing my best to maneuver you away from the front windows, for your sake as much as for mine. And I was saying "please," not "squeeze." Furthermore, I am *not* hiding. I was not home

74

when you came and so could not have been "peeking out." I am not afraid of Mr. Brud. And I do not want you to forgive me. I want you to pay your rent.

Andrew Whittaker

The Whittaker Company

¶

Dear Vikki,

I think publicity is the first thing, or one of the first things. It seems to me important to give people the impression that something is happening, even if nothing is happening. What do you think of this?

Andy

PRESS RELEASE

Soap, the nationally acclaimed literary journal, has made public its plans for an annual literary festival. Though rumors of such a festival have been bandied about in literary circles for several months, this is the first official statement from the magazine itself.

At a crowded press conference in a downtown hotel, Andrew Whittaker, editor and publisher of *Soap* and one of the coordinators for the event, announced that the theme for this year's festival will be "Inside the Outside." Mr. Whittaker explained: "We want to increase the dialogue between contemporary cutting-edge writers and the general public, to try and bring an end to the hostility and suspicion prevalent on both sides. It's a two-way street." At another point he described the conflict as a "big misunderstanding" and a "nothing burger."

Mr. Whittaker says he expects this year's event to draw "three dozen plus" writers and poets from across the nation and Europe. Unlike other literary festivals, which, according to Whittaker, have been "proliferating like fleas" in small cities around the country, none of the writers showcased at the Soap Festival will be publicity-hungry wannabes. "I'll personally see to that," he said. He declined to name the wannabes, saying only that "they know who they are." A tall burly man, he seemed to be at home in front of the jostling crowd of journalists, joking at times with a young female reporter who appeared thoroughly charmed by his wit and exuberance. While he declined to give a firm figure concerning the number of visitors expected, when pressed he said he would "not be surprised" to see "twelve or thirteen thousand" over the five days of the festival, adding "there are going to be traffic problems for sure."

In addition to attending (for a small fee) any of numerous workshops, lectures, readings, and book signings, visitors will be able to stroll freely about in what Whittaker calls a "county-fair atmosphere," with live music, free balloons, and stalls selling book-related novelties and souvenirs.

Saturday will bring the potluck "Picnic in the Park" to which the general public is invited, followed by a firework display after sunset. Sunday, the fifth and final day, will witness the festival's culminating event: the presentation by Mr. Whittaker of The Soap Lifetime Achievement Award to a literary figure of world renown, followed by a formal dinner and dance at the sumptuous Coolidge Ballroom. Whittaker declined to reveal the name of the recipient of this year's award, saying cryptically, "You'll find out when the little bird sings." He declined to say what bird he was referring to. The award itself will be a framed photograph of Marilyn Monroe in a bubble bath. Whittaker described the photo as "about the size of a breakfast tray."

¶

Maria,

Don't bother cleaning upstairs. I have a touch of something and have decided to stay in bed. Also, please do not run the vacuum. There's a broom in the basement closet. Do the best you can. I apologize for the mess in the bathroom. You may leave that if it seems too much. Do not throw out any bottles that still have something in them. Gracias

¶

Dear Jolie,

What do you think of this?

I am standing in a street, looking up at the door of a brick building, a rundown apartment house or tenement of some kind. Some of the windowpanes have been knocked out and replaced by pieces of brown cardboard. Several metal trashcans, bent and overflowing with garbage, are lined up at the curb. They look fake, like trashcans in a comic book, put there to show that this is "a place of poverty." I have the feeling of having "arrived at last" at the end of a long search for just this building. Lifting my feet with difficulty—they feel weighted with lead—I climb the several steps to the door. The wood around the latch is scarred and splintered, as if someone had tried to break in. I expect it to be locked and am surprised when it opens to a gentle push, as of its own accord.

I step directly into a large low-ceilinged room, like a church basement. The walls are yellow, and the light in the room is oddly yellow as well. It occurs to me, in the dream, that this color is commonly referred to as "urinous," a word that, in the dream, I find comical. The air is thick, almost liquid. On a green sofa in the center of the room sits a very small man, a midget or a dwarf. He is watching television on a tiny black-and-white set that sits on a straight-backed chair in front of the sofa. There is no other furniture in the room. The dwarf, or midget, is middle-aged, broad-shouldered and stocky, with a flaccid, characterless face. He is neatly dressed in a dark pin-striped suit, a bow tie, and a bowler hat. I'm aware that he has escaped from a circus, and that I'm supposed to capture him and take him back there. I know this is an "important task," and the prospect of failure fills me with anxiety.

The dwarf takes no notice of me when I enter, but goes on watching the television and laughing loudly. He even laughs at the ads. I am wondering how to get his attention, when suddenly he glances up—I think he has heard my thoughts—and pats the sofa cushion next to him. I understand he wants me to sit and watch television with him. I shake my head no. At the same time I hold up a short piece of rope. He sees it, and his eyes widen in a grotesque parody of fear. Then he sticks his tongue out at me, slithers off the sofa, snatches up the little TV set, and holding it in the crook of one arm, the cord and plug trailing on the floor behind him, scampers into another room. I'm astonished at how fast he can move, his short legs whirling in a blur beneath him like a figure in a cartoon. I struggle after him, my own feet still terribly heavy, into what looks like a room in a cheap hotel. I feel as if I'm swimming in the thick urinous air, and

I move my arms like a swimmer. I know he's hiding in the room somewhere. I search under the bed, in all the drawers, behind the window curtains, even back of a cracked mirror on the dresser. Finally, I catch sight of the television's cord protruding like a rat's tail beneath a door. I yank the door open and spy him crouching at the back of a deep closet. He's fiddling with the knobs on his TV, which sits propped on a pile of women's shoes in front of him. I drag him, giggling, out by his feet. I'm trying to stuff him head first into a cloth sack when he begins to scream.

I woke up to the whine of a garbage truck in the street. The dream was tenacious, and all day long snatches of it have been breaking in on my thoughts. It had an odor of anxiety clinging to it at first, but that has dissipated finally.

My eyes are not better. Among the things I brought up from the basement were a half-dozen plastic tarps, and I've nailed those over the living room windows to cut the glare. The room is now wonderfully blue.

I saw Fran on Monroe Street a few days ago, as I was leaving the bank, and I followed her, forcing her to walk faster and faster until, in evident panic, she ran up the steps of a house and beat with both fists on the door. I passed by without even a glance in her direction, as if I had no idea that she was in front of me. I wonder if she even knew the people in that house.

Love,
Andy

¶

Adam had come to this place to be alone, to be alone and not think, and to wait for his younger brother Saul. He thought of Saul and spit. The spit landed on the floor, where it formed a whitish mound in the dust. He remembered Saul's mocking eyes, his greasy hair, his crooked goatee, and his snakeskin boots. He lay back on the mattress, fell back heavily upon it. He could hear the wind soughing in the tall grass in the yard. He could hear the ragged cries of the gulls wheeling along the lakeshore, white handkerchiefs turned and tossed by the wind. He thought of other shores, other birds. He thought of other grass . . .

Flo leaped from the high truck cab to the ground, slammed the door, and walked to the back of the truck. She dropped the rear gate, dragged out the two rough-sawn timbers that served as a ramp, and jammed the bottom ends into the dirt, stamping them firmly in with her foot. She then carefully maneuvered the green John Deere mower down the ramp and onto the gravel at the side of the road. She did not look in the direction of the house, but she could feel his gaze upon her.

For the whump of the tailgate had roused him from the bed where he had lain all morning, while the sun climbed in the sky and the noise of the gulls grew ever more insistent, mingled as it was with the distant barking of a dog. He had been lying with his eyes open staring up at the yellowish water stains on the plaster ceiling. He had managed to pick out the outlines of Britain, along with several stains that looked amazingly like giant cauliflowers, and above the window he had found a large frog with a tennis racquet in its mouth. This last had made him remember the frogs at Wellfleet and the wonderful clay courts they had there. And this had made him remember yet other things: the house, the black Mercedes, and Glenda sunning in the deckchair. He remembered walking out from the house, a drink in his hand. He had stood over her and seen his own reflection in her sunglasses, twice. She had removed the glasses. Her laughing eyes had flickered uneasily. He was reflected in them as well, though strangely small. "When I drove up last night," he said, "there was a man standing on the deck."

Now once again he thought of the figure on the deck, a man in an overcoat, and he looked for it among the scattered stains on the ceiling. But the stain was not on the ceiling! He turned in the bed and coughed uneasily. The silhouetted shape had seemed strangely familiar, though wrapped in the large coat it might have been anyone. Anyone! But there had seemed to be something hanging from its mouth, a piece of toast perhaps, or a dark goatee! The figure had turned and strode with rapid strides out onto the beach, to vanish in the rising fog. For reasons obscure even to himself Adam had said nothing to Glenda that night. He had waited for her to speak first, hoping against hope that she would say something to allay his worst fear. She could have said—and he would have believed her, he would have forced himself to believe her— that she had just received a visit from a neighbor, from old half-crippled Carl Billcamp next door or from Susan, their painter friend, who in an overcoat could look like a man, or even that he had imagined it all. Anything, even madness, would have been better than the coiled silence which had lain between them all that day, somnolent and menacing like some dreadful beast that neither dared disturb.

The whump of the tailgate crashed in upon these memories like a fist crashing through a windowpane.

¶

Really, Dahlberg,

You are really overreacting. I don't need a list of all the sharp things in your store and you should stop thinking about them. You have to find someone you can talk to, someone who can help you put things into perspective. And I don't think it tasteful of you, at this point, to start referring to *Soap* as a "dingy little magazine."

Andy

¶

Dear Fern,

I have the new poems and the pictures. The poems are much stronger than the ones you submitted before, occasionally quite striking in the way they capture the particularities of physical sensation—walking barefoot in the dew-sparkled morning and stepping on the "diamond-soft pins" of new-cut grass, squeezing a bar of water-softened soap and feeling "the greasy slithering of the soft white flesh" oozing between your fingers and recalling your dead grandmother making Christmas cookies, her wizened hand in the Crisco, etc. And you have a real gift for animate description, as in the poem about the dying bear. But sorry, still not quite what we are looking for. As for illustrating your earlier "Self Portrait in Five" with photos, I don't see the point of that. It does nothing for the poem. And anyway, *Soap* doesn't publish photos—much too expensive—in case that's what you are thinking.

Let me also say, while I'm being frank, that there seems to me something a trifle "off" about the pictures themselves. Nothing technical like lighting or focus. I am thinking more of the puzzling expression you wear in some of them—a pinched, strained, almost scowling look. I don't mean to be wounding, and I am not suggesting that you are anything but an attractive young woman (on the contrary), but I would not be exaggerating if I described you as looking "extremely sour" in these pictures. They certainly present a very different and, I have to say, less appealing person than the girl I saw in the snapshots you sent me before. The new photos, it seems to me, advertise bitterness and disappointment, as if *those* were the true themes of your work, even while your poem is saying just the opposite. At first I took them as reflections of your unhappiness at home, but now, having looked at them again, I see another explanation, one that is disappointingly banal, I am afraid, having to do with the camera's automatic timer.

Consider the shot you pair with the section "Up and Down." I imagine the following sequence. After setting the timer for, let's say, a minute and a half, you take a seat on the swing's little wooden platform and push off. Clutching a rope in each hand, you clamber to your feet. Now you vigorously agitate your pelvic and lumbar portions, if I may put it that way, along with your arms and shoulders. But the swing moves painfully slow; to force it higher you must "pump" with your knees. This would be great fun were it a matter of swinging any old way, just swinging for the hell of it, but you can't let yourself relax and enjoy the ride, for even as you carry out the fore-described complex set of synchronized movements you are counting down the seconds with chronometric exactitude, perhaps saying to yourself, "one-Mississippi, two-Mississippi." Your aim is to regulate the tempo of the swing in such a way that it will begin to fall from the pinnacle of its backward arc at the exact instant the camera's shutter has been set to open, at which point the wind will lift your dress just as you describe it in the poem. No wonder you look sour! Your camera captures the precise contour of every muscle in your calves and thighs (I am guessing you play a wicked game of tennis), but it also, alas, accentuates all the telltale muscles in your face, which is now stamped with the pinched expression of someone doing difficult sums in her head. Perhaps "sour" is not the word. A better choice might be "desperate."

I am guessing something similar was going on in the picture you pair with the section beginning "It's morning, hurry"—a rather nice piece of writing by the way, with the image of the sun "razoring" open the face of the day. In that one, after setting the timer, I picture you jumping into bed and slipping quickly beneath the sheet. And now you must lie there, limbs outstretched, and count down the seconds, listening, perhaps, to the faint hum of the timer a few feet away on its tripod—it sounds like an insect in your ear screaming "18, 17, 16 . . ."—until at long last the moment arrives to toss the sheet into the air, where it will billow cloudlike above you at the instant of the click. I wonder how many times you tried that one before getting it right!

On a practical level, should you decide to continue with this project, I suggest you get a human assistant to operate the camera for you. It would be nice if all the photographs were at the level of the one with you straddling the porch railing. Your expression in that one is anything but sour. "Alluring" is the better word. But of course you know that. You might send some of the less "racy" poems to your local newspaper. Small-town weeklies, always desperate for copy, are sometimes quite welcoming to local artists.

Best wishes and good look,

Andy Whittaker,

Editor at *Soap*

¶

Dear Maria,

Please accept my heartfelt apologies for what happened last week. When you didn't show up on Tuesday, it finally dawned on me that you are truly offended. When I called you into the room, I had been sitting at my desk writing since before dawn and I had completely forgotten that I was not wearing any clothes. You probably find that difficult to believe, since I know you come from a culture in which people like to stay buttoned up, even at their desks probably, or zipped up, if that is what they have. But up here, especially in one's own house, it is easy to forget. I suppose I made it worse by laughing, for which I am also sorry. I hope you will come back.

Mr. Whittaker

¶

Dear Jolie,

Here's a postcard showing the new shopping center. I am writing it in the living room, which is piled high with boxes and awash in the blue light of tarps. I am very happy with the light, though not with the shopping center or the boxes. The radio sits on a stack of boxes beside me, and I switched it on a moment ago in the crazy outside hope of hearing Billie Holiday sing "Am I Blue." I told myself that if this were actually to happen it would mean the world is all right. Of course, what I got instead was a hideous blast of rock and roll.

Much love,

Andy

¶

To the Editor:

Enough! For many years the *Current* has honed a well-deserved reputation for ignorance and Philistinism, but your most recent foray into the field of letters takes the cake. While your article ("Our City Shaking and Moving") purports to be a "literary roundup" of "our best writers and where to read them," what we really get is a fawning puff piece on *The Art News*, which your reporter describes as "irreverent" and "lively." To which I say, "lively my keister!" It is a well-known fact that *The Art News* is nothing more than the in-house journal for a tiny clique of very conventional, very middle-class writers and painters, most of them ladies. "Semi-literate rag" would be a too charitable description of that publication. This reader would like to object that, since the article is explicitly presented as a "roundup," it is under some obligation to rope in *all* the cows, including, I concede, such spavined, mange-stricken little doggies as *The Art News*. But *does* it bring them all in? It does not. For example, how many times does the article mention Andrew Whittaker's *Soap*? The astonishing answer is *not even once*. Not one small mention of a publication that is without doubt the most imposing literary venue in our state, publishing pioneers like

Adolphus Stepwell, E. Sterling Macaw, and Marsha Beddoes-Varlinsky. Have your readers heard of any of those writers? Probably not, and this is precisely why we need people like Andrew Whittaker, our one local writer whose name might elicit something other than "huh?" on the sidewalks of Madison or Ann Arbor. For ten years Whittaker has gone about his work, without remuneration, sustained by the conviction that he is serving a higher purpose, oblivious to the winks and snickers raining upon him from, among other places, the pages of your newspaper. Now, as if goaded by his continued indifference, you see fit to pepper him with silence. How loathsome!

Sincerely,

Warden Hawktiter, MD

¶

Dear Anita,

I've not been able to get your letter out of my thoughts. I sit down to work at my novel, and I find myself in imaginary conversation with you. It's O.K. that you want to have "not the slightest whiff" of me in the future. I am not going to fly to Ithaca and howl on your doormat. But I am astonished at your distortions of the past. While it might not meet the current demands of your *amour propre*, it is still OUR past and not yours to fiddle around with. I was amazed that you could write the following: "As far as I am concerned, *nothing* happened during that weekend to make me want to reminisce now. I don't recall damp sheets or lurid lighting on my 'semaphores' (God, you're awful!). What I remember is a very young and very frightened girl trapped in a squalid motel room with a bullying neurotic." You *frightened*? Isn't "frolicsome" the word you want? *Whose* idea was the wicker basket? I'm sorry to be crude about this, but the person I was with in that "squalid room" was a rambunctious bawdy athletic *broad*. It's obvious you meant your letter to be as hurtful as possible. And it was. How could you bring yourself to call my reminiscences "erotic treacle"? I am not going to forgive you for that.

Andy

¶

Dear Jolie,

Last Friday night I was lying in bed, still awake, when two firemen hammered on the door to tell me the Spalding Street building had burned to the ground. It had happened earlier that afternoon, but it took them till almost midnight to notify me, because I don't have a telephone. We are fortunate that no one was in the building at the time; I don't know what would happen if we had a lot of grieved relatives suing. The insurance money, such as it is, will all go to the bank, so don't imagine that a big wad is going to sail through your mail slot. You of course hated the building for no good reason, just because you don't like asbestos siding. Still, its demise means your next check is going to be smaller. I hope you are not going to argue about this. If you don't believe me, send Fender out to look at the ashes.

I haven't slept since then, or at any rate that's how it feels to me, though I must have dozed off occasionally, twenty winks, if not forty. How else could I still be functioning even at the modest level at which I am functioning? I must be sleeping without knowing it, though I can't imagine when it occurs. Probably not in bed at night, since that's when I am most acutely conscious of being awake. I spend a lot of time looking at television. I suppose I might be sleeping then. By evening I am terribly tired. I am happy to be tired, thinking that now at last I'll sleep. I drag myself up the steps and climb into bed. I stretch myself out like a corpse, and *pop* go the eyelids. It's horrible. I can almost hear the noise the lids make as they slam up against the roof of my eye sockets. At the same time I feel my body going rigid, my fingers and toes splay, the muscles in my neck bulge. I lie like that for hours, until I can't stand it any longer, and then I get up and wander around the house, the empty, absolutely silent house, surrounded by the screams of crickets. At those times I wish I had a telephone so I could call somebody up and yell at them.

I don't care about the Spalding Street building, as a building, any more than you do. But its loss means that another trickle of income has been staunched, and I'm that much closer to complete bankruptcy. I don't see why you can't get a real job, at least until I can put things here back on their feet. The money I send you would just about do it. You can be an actress next year. Why can't you be something else this year? After all, you already know how to type. I am struggling. I have several projects, but they all need time to bear fruit. I am working on a new novel, one I have been thinking about for a while, aimed at a wider public this time. I don't see why I can't do it without compromising my principles.

Yes, I did have a maid. She was coming once a week, and she hardly stayed long enough to make even a small dent in the mess, which is really like a nation of its own. I had a maid not because I had money to throw away but because I am now considered a charity case. I am considered this by people who ought to know, who have to deal professionally, on a daily basis, with cases like that, like mine. I let her go because I could no longer afford the sandwiches she ate for lunch. After poking around in the mess for an hour or so, while making little complaining noises in her native tongue, she would go home or back to church or wherever they go, and I would open the refrigerator and discover she had eaten my supper. I have to drink the cheapest whiskey now, and I never have wine. I tried to get the firemen to come in and have a drink with me. Do you ever have the thought that we might get back together when all this is over?

Love,

Andy

p.s. I don't know what I mean by "all this."

¶

Dear Fern,

I had not expected to hear back from you so soon. It is really too bad you were able to dig up only one old issue of the magazine, and too bad it had to be that one. Your obviously tongue-in-cheek assertion that you were "horribly shocked" suggests to me that you were *in fact* a little bit shocked. You can't say I didn't warn you! Even so, I would not have picked an issue containing Nadine's "Crotch Poems" as the best introduction to the sort of writing we want. Nadine is quite the exception. And it's too bad the same issue also contains my "Meditations of an Old

Pornographer." I do hope you understand that this piece was meant as a satire of a certain type of person, a lonely, aging, and desperate "loser" (to use a really nasty expression). It is, of course, a literary fabrication, a piece of fiction, and not a description of the sort of things I personally think about while I am in the tub. I insist on this point because of your remark that I am a "funny man." To give you a more rounded picture of what we are all about, I enclose some other back issues.

Your poetry just keeps getting better—stronger, more confident, and edgier. Really amazing progress. I was, quite sincerely, astonished by some of them, in particular "Banjo, Bozo" and "The Circus Tent of Sex." I'd like to include those two in our April issue. This is bold stuff from someone your age, and it's sure to make some people uncomfortable when they find out just how young you are. But I suppose you've figured out by now that we don't pull punches at *Soap*.

I'm relieved you did not take amiss my bit of advice about the self-timer. At least I hope you didn't, and that you are joking when you accuse me of saying you look like a "sour person"? You know I was perfectly sincere in my remarks about your alluring aspects. Why wouldn't I be?

I observe, in closing, that the poem "To an Old Writer" carries a dedication to me. I am flattered, and will print that one too, space permitting. I do, however, have a small bone to pick here: the stanza in which you imagine my "care-furrowed face" looking over your shoulder while you are writing suggests to me that you think I am *old*. While it's true that I am an old hand at the writing game, I am not at all old in the doddering sense. If you and I were to stroll down a street together, for example, no one could mistake you for my daughter! And despite those muscled gams of yours, I imagine you'd find me more than a match on a tennis court, were we ever to meet on one.

Yours truly,
Andy

¶

Mr. Fontini—

I never suggested Archimedes or anyone else was taking baths with Mrs. Fontini, which, if you think about it, would scarcely be possible for anyone larger than a spaniel. And no, I don't know his first name. Instead of worrying about the "Greek shit" in your bathtub, you should worry about sending me the money you owe. Forthwith. Or I go to court.

Andrew Whittaker
The Whittaker Company

¶

Dear Mr. Carmichael,

I have your letter telling me of Mama's death. Of course, that death was not a surprise. In life's dreary cavalcade of adjectives, "dead" does seem to follow hard on "old" with mournful regularity. Have you ever thought of it that way? So it was not, as I said, a surprise, and neither was it a jolt in the usual I-have-to-sit-down sort of way, but it was a little shock. I was shocked (slightly) not that she was dead—as remarked above, she was old, etc.—but at how little I cared. It was not that I didn't give a damn, I didn't give an *anything*. You will say that I am experiencing that numbness which always precedes grief—I can almost hear you saying it, almost see that peculiarly unpleasant pursing thing you do with your lips—but you are wrong. I don't feel in the least numb. If anything I feel a whiff giddy. Two days later, and I catch myself smiling when I think of it, which is not very often. I think, "Mama has popped off," and I grin.

Now back to the pursing thing. I suppose you feel this puckering bit adds gravitas to your mien, renders it harmonious with solemn phrases like "I regret that your dear mother has passed away." I would like to believe you are doing it in order to suppress the giggles, but I know that is a long shot. You have been kind to Mama and me, so I think I should tell you that you are not fooling anyone. When someone begins a sentence with "I regret," I always want to say "Oh, pooh!" I suppose you think that is very cynical of me. Why don't you think instead that it is very *sincere* of me? After all, the distance between the two is no wider than a cat's whisker.

Though I have made efforts to conceal it (for the sake of other people really, who would otherwise find my presence uncomfortable), I did not much care for Mama. She was a stupid, disagreeable, selfish woman. She was an awful snob as well. And now she is gone. What a mystery life and death are. How shall we ever get to the bottom of it? Please do not send me any of her personal belongings except jewelry. As for burial or cremation, do whichever is least expensive.

Sincerely,
Andrew Whittaker

¶

Dear Jolie,

Mama's dead. I feel utterly unbereft. And yet I can't stop thinking of her. Little things, like her passion for the 1812 Overture and the hideous yellow pants she wore to play golf.

I got the fire inspector's report today. It was arson, as I thought from the beginning. It seems the fire started in four different places at more or less the same time. Those fellows are quite cunning, the way they can go through a pile of charred wood and brick and come up with a plausible story. If I could go through the ruins of my life and come up with a plausible story, we'd be in business. Furthermore the whole Brud family has disappeared. I can see that big homely woman striding through the house with a blowtorch, blasting a spot here, a spot there, while the little toad-like husband hops behind her croaking, "Darling, are you sure this is a good idea?" I've come to expect very little of people, but this is a family that I went out of my way to be kind to. The clouds of ingratitude rain fire upon us. Is that it?

Love,

Andy

¶

In the desert. A woman with two men. A man with two women. A boy, one of the crowd of children, is lying on his back in the hot sand, sweltering in his dark-blue sailor suit. A man and a woman look down at him, eyes filled with pity, and then glance quickly at each other. The boy will remember this later. He will recall that glance as somehow "inestimably peculiar." The man is the man with two women. The woman is the woman with two men. A complex web is being woven.

There is also a woman with a cat, and two women with one dog. They fight. The man and the woman who had been looking down at the boy, it could be a lifetime ago, draw apart from the others, to stand together, but not touching, on the sandy bank of the river. Behind them, sounds of continuous quarreling. Looking out at the water, speaking to the man, though not turning her head to face him, the woman says in a voice without inflection, and yet, for this very reason, charged with meaning, "Through the desert of tedium flows a river of dread." Horrified, the man realizes that this is true.

¶

Dear Harold,

You are probably right, I *am* working too hard. It's difficult to keep things in proportion sometimes. Like everyone else I have my up days and down days. But I discern a trend: the trend is downward. I always used to have an orderly mind, never put things in jars without labels, and would scold Jolie for keeping important papers under magnets on the refrigerator. I hated opening the door and having some unpaid bill or vital phone number sail loopingly off in the direction of the floor, sometimes in a slanting dive that would send it slithering beneath the refrigerator from whence it would have to be extracted with a broom handle. I sometimes had difficulty containing my rage when this happened, if Jolie was not home and I had to be the one to get down on my knees and bang about with the broom. I finally had no choice but to take all the magnets off.

Furthermore, I always had files. Whatever wasn't filed in a labeled folder in one of five metal cabinets (in drawers I kept so well oiled they slid in and out with scarcely a whisper) was filed in my mind in tiny cabinets arranged along the walls of my skull. I always at every instant of the day knew exactly where my toothbrush or my copy of *Tropic of Cancer* was. I wanted something, I had only to put out my hand and grab it. So how is it possible that I have started losing things left and right? That is not in keeping with my character. You surely remember my character. I have a tidy nature. You remember how tidy I kept our dorm room. You remember how I made you stand on the bed while I mopped the floor. I'm afraid something organic is going on in my brain, due perhaps to a severe lack of oxygen. The brain uses twenty percent of the body's total supply of oxygen. That's a lot more than one would think, considering what else is going on in there, the organic wheels and pistons churning and grinding all the time, every little cell screaming for a slice of the pie. I have to take deep breaths all the time now.

I was sure I had placed my cup of coffee—the first of the day—on a box in the living room. It was a pale blue mug with daisies; there was steam coming out of it. The coffee stood just below the halfway mark, or would have had there been a mark; it was level with the bottom daisy. The box on which I had placed it was the topmost box in the second stack of boxes to the left of the front windows. It previously had contained four dozen Scott towels. This information was displayed in large blue letters on the side of the box. I say all this to show that I have an *exact picture* of the location in which I had placed the cup. I had been holding it in my left hand. In my right I held four small galvanized nails, and I placed those on the box as well, right next to the cup. They clinked against it. I can see my hand as I reached out to place the cup on the box, the knob of my wristbone inching forth from its hiding place in my sleeve, the hairs on my wrist springing erect as they escape the pressure of the cloth. That was just before going down to the basement in search of a hammer with which to nail tarps up over the front windows. The sun was very bright. The tarps were blue.

That was ten mornings ago. It was late in the afternoon three days later when I saw the coffee cup again. I was sitting on a plastic milk box in the upstairs hall. I was pulling books out of one of the two large bookcases up there and placing them in boxes. I had clasped a row of small paperbacks between my palms and was lifting them, still in a row, off the shelf, and there behind them—I almost wrote, "crouching there behind them"—was the cup. It had been three and a half days, the milk had curdled, and a dead roach was floating on the scummed surface. I noticed then that one of the books behind which the cup had hidden was Peterson's *A Field Guide to Insects*. While I remember shaking with laughter at this coincidence, in retrospect I am not able to see anything funny in it. The cup had been cleverly concealed, the entire shelf of books moved forward a couple of inches so the row of books in front of the cup would not stand out. I poured the coffee out in the bathroom sink, forcing the roach down through the drain sieve with the handle of a toothbrush.

And then there's the case of the lost notebook. It was one in which I had been jotting bits and pieces for a couple of stories I am working on. The house was really quite bare, most of the smaller things—books, pictures, most of the clothing, most of the *debris*—packed in boxes in the living room, rugs rolled up and shoved against the walls, empty drawers stacked on top of dressers, etc. Few hiding places of the usual sort remained except under all the papers, photos, and magazines strewn on the desk and floor, and this was the first place I looked. It was not there. After combing the house up and down, I became convinced that in my haste to get everything packed up I had inadvertently stuck the notebook in one of the boxes. I could not see any other explanation. But which box? I knew it had to be in one of the half dozen or so I had packed since last seeing it a few days before, yet I had no way of distinguishing the suspect boxes from several dozen similar ones with which they had now become mingled. You see, whenever I finish a box I don't simply place it on top of a stack, heave it up there and just walk off. Or rather, I do that, but then I always come back later and move it. I often rearrange my boxes, for a variety of reasons, and I must have restacked them all several times before it dawned on me that the notebook was almost certainly in one of them, and by that time there was no way I could possibly *deduce*, just by standing there thinking about it, which of the many boxes (at this point they were more than forty) was the culprit. From that point of view they were identical, and all I could think to do was unpack them one at a time. Once I had decided on this course of action, I tore through them like a madman, flinging the contents helter-skelter onto the floor, along with huge quantities of balled-up newspaper. The hunt took most of a day and by the end of it the entire surface of the living room was covered with *stuff*. And it's that way still; I haven't had the heart to repack any of it. I had emptied every single box, I had individually examined every item, shaken every book before flinging it, all in vain. Then yesterday evening, just as I was preparing to sit down to supper—

a salami and tomato sandwich and a small whiskey—I noticed the notebook lying in full view on the kitchen table.

It's interesting that you have taken up writing. Who hasn't these days? I'll be glad to look over your MS, if that is what you're asking.

Andy

SEPTEMBER

Dear Bob, Eric, and Juan,

I have received another complaint about the noise. You will have to turn it down after 10 or find another place. Wear clothes when you go to the basement with your laundry. Think of the people in the other apartments, who are not as young as you are, have to get up and go to work, and are religious to boot. None of that is their fault.

Sincerely,
Andrew Whittaker
The Whittaker Company

¶

Dear Fern,

I have the new poems and photographs.

They came in the same mail as a letter telling me of my mother's death. It was an expected death, one that mercy would have sent sooner, though it has left a small gap nonetheless. The world tilts at an odder angle, and at night I dream of boats.

So I guessed correctly—the self timer was the problem. The new photographs are *much* improved, so much so that I made the mistake of propping one of them up on my desk, the one of you with the cat on the sofa. I ought to have known better. I am, as you have probably guessed, a single man, practically the archetypical "confirmed bachelor," and the abrupt appearance on my desk of a large photograph showing an attractive young lady on a sofa, in an attitude that can only be described as languid, provoked a spate of good-natured teasing from some of the staff, the older women especially. They are loveable old hens in the main, so

I tried not to show my irritation, but needless to say, your pictures now resides harmlessly in a drawer.

I am not sure I understand what you mean by "loosening it up"—what *it* are you referring to?—but I do sense more spontaneity in the poems and the photos, and this I consider a good thing, since spontaneity can induce surprises. I myself enjoy being surprising, becoming startling just when people think I am asleep, or, contrariwise, falling asleep while they are waiting to be surprised. Please convey my compliments to your school friend. It's the true photographer who can pick out the exact right moment to press the button. I suppose she knows the work of Cartier-Bresson, the best of the slice-of-life school, where knowing when to push the button is pretty much all there is to it. If not, I'd be happy to pass along an edition I have here at the office, as that stuff doesn't really interest me.

I couldn't help noticing that, in addition to the relaxed smile on your face, you have made other changes to the photos—I mean, of course, the garment you have on in the shot that shows you throwing off the covers, if "garment" is not too big a word for such an exiguous item. I would not have thought you could buy a thing like that in Rufus. You're a very remarkable girl indeed. Such contradictions! Talking to a friend the other day, I described your earlier poems as "childlike and ribald." I hope you don't mind. I don't know what to call these new ones. What *have* you been reading? I suggest you don't hand any of *these* in to old Mr. Crawford! And in your person too, there is the contrast between your face, wide-eyed and youthful, and the rest of you, which, as you surely know, seems amazingly developed. Where are your parents while all this is happening?

I am delighted you found my "Meditations of an Old Pornographer" exciting, even on a second reading, though I did wince at one thing you said. I called the story a literary fabrication, it is true, but that does not mean, as you assume, that it is therefore "insincere" or "just some made-up stuff." In an extenuated and yet profound sense every writer of fiction has to become, indeed must be already, every character he creates. So *of course* I harbor somewhere, if harbor is the word, impulses and desires similar to those of the old pornographer, including the ones you call "fantastically kinky," by which I suppose you mean the soap and cucumber thing or the stuff with the rubber band. Though I don't want to pry, I would be interested in knowing, when you say the story was exciting, whether you mean a general sort of literary excitement or something else. One is always uncertain, and of course always curious, about how people of the opposite sex are going to take things.

So you really like Dahlberg Stint's work. I had forgotten the issue containing his piece was among the ones I had sent you. Sorry, though, I can't send anything else of his—the story you read is the only thing we've published, or that anyone has published, as far as I know. You are right—it is intense stuff, though I wouldn't go so far as to call him an incredible genius. These days I think of him more as a sad case. The stuff he has submitted lately is so bad some of us are convinced he couldn't possibly have written those hardware stories. Of course, we'd love to know who the real author is, but we hesitate to ask Stint directly, since he seems to be only marginally sane.

If you have taught tennis at summer camp, you must be good at it. I play a fair game myself, though some people won't play me on the grounds that I am too aggressive.

I have been publishing *Soap* for seven years. It has meant personal sacrifice and a lot of drudgery, and many times I have wanted to throw the whole thing up and concentrate instead on my own work, which currently sits in neglected heaps on my desk at home, in boxes shoved under beds, and in the case of a couple of short stories, in a filing-cabinet drawer which is stuck hopelessly shut. But then, just when I am saying to myself, "Andy, why not chuck the whole thing?" I come across a talent like yours, and it all seems worthwhile again. I felt I ought to tell you this.

With contributors all over the country, plus conferences and lectures, I am forced to travel about rather more than I would like. I can't tell you how many poems and stories I have started while sitting in hotels and airports. Looking at my schedule I see that next month has me passing by car just a stone's throw from Rufus. It occurs to me that I could stop by and say hello, perhaps meet you somewhere in town. You might like to join me for coffee or lunch. I hope you won't feel I am being forward. I could bring my racquet. What do you think?

Sincerely,

Andy Whittaker

¶

Dear Dahlberg,

I think you would find it a lot easier to get people to like you if you made an effort to think of someone besides yourself. I've gone out on a limb for you. You can't imagine the kind of shit I had to put up with after publishing your work. While that does not mean that I regret having done it, it was still a lot of shit and you might show some gratitude. IT HURTS AND DISTRESSES ME to read the stuff you keep sending. I think you should be made aware that I am not a young man. I am under tremendous pressure all the time. I have noises in my chest. So why don't you just fucking lighten up?

Andy

¶

The whump of the tailgate startled Adam from his reveries, shredding the web of his thought much as an orb weaver's intricate pattern, stretched in dewy splendor athwart a woodland path, is shredded by the dull face of an insensitive hiker. He heard the long scraping sound made by the heavy timbers sliding from the back of the truck. This was a sound he knew well, for as a younger, stronger man, more integrated personally, he had worked in construction, and for a moment he imagined he was back on the job. He sprang from the stained and lumpy mattress, half expecting to find his tool belt with his rip-claw Estwing hammer lying on a chair next to his steel-toed work boots. This was, alas, but another trick played by a cruel mind on its hapless owner. In the past three days he had eaten nothing but some berries he had found growing wild along the shore, and now, weakened by hunger, his legs gave way beneath him and he fell numbly to the floor, striking his head against the iron bed with a dull metallic thud. Out in the yard Flo heard the noise, but thought it was an eighty-pound sack of hog feed being tossed to the ground, for that is what it most resembled.

Adam must have lost consciousness, for when he opened his eyes again the air was filled with the throaty growl of a large lawnmower. Cursing his own weakness, he staggered to his feet and stumbled over to the window. He was filled with a silent incohesive rage. She was already on her fifth pass, and a wide swath of mowed meadow grass now stretched bleakly between the shack and the road. He recognized the girl on the bicycle, the girl who had been on a bicycle the last time he saw her. Now she sat perched on the high metal seat of a big green mower and with flicks of her wrist was deftly steering it this way and that. He noticed she was mowing in back and forth passes, which required her to turn the machine completely around at the end of each pass, rather than using the more efficient method of mowing in continuous circles of ever-decreasing radii. As he watched, the tractor suddenly lurched to a halt, the engine moaned in almost human agony, and died with a little puff of white smoke from beneath the engine cowl. "Damn," she chirped, and her voice was clear and bright as the water of the great lake flashing in postmatinal splendor behind her. She hopped lithely to the ground. She knelt on all fours, bending low and curving her back as she reached far under the chassis in order to pull a tenacious mass of thorny brambles from the drive shaft. He noticed she was wearing cut-off jeans. He noticed the sinewy calves and muscular thighs and the small tight buttocks. And once again something tugged at his memory.

She was aware of his gaze upon her. It was oddly warm and moist, as if he were caressing her with his eyeballs, and she shivered with mingled fear and pleasure. Flo had lived long enough to know the terrible hunger lurking in the eyes of womanless men. She had felt it on the lonely streets of Kearney, Nebraska, where, as a young girl away from home for the first time, she had worked for the post office as a substitute mail carrier in training, while earning a degree in English from the university. Oh, but that was long ago, before her mother's slow death from ovarian cancer and her father's accident had brought her back to the farm, to the long days of backbreaking labor and the lonely nights reading Chaucer in her room, and now the sick chickens! Though she would not admit it to anyone, she missed the gazes. She had felt a strange excitement at the knowledge that the men, sitting on benches sipping from brown paper sacks or leaning from the high cabs of cross-country rigs idling at traffic lights, were undressing her in the streets. She had been aware of the way the strap of the mail bag crossed between her breasts, pulling her shirt taut against them. And she also had been aware that through some mysterious action at a distance she was causing tumescences and spasms in the bodies of those who saw her.

And now, as she worked at the tangle of briar and weed wrapping the drive shaft, she felt it again. Adam had come out onto the porch and was leaning heavily against the wall.

She walked over, wiping her hands on the back of her shorts. She stood at the bottom of the steps looking up at him. She noticed the goose egg on his forehead.

"You're hurt," she said. She wanted to go closer, but something held her back, for she was wary of this stranger standing before her.

He did not answer right away, but continued to look at her, his eyes moving up and down her slim body. She felt his eyes removing her garments one by one. She noticed a change in the cries of the gulls. "Just a bump," he said at last.

Now she noticed the berry stains on his hands and mouth. She remembered a Chippewa legend. She lifted her arms as his eyes clasped the bottom of her t-shirt and lifted it. The gulls cried demonically.

God, what shit!!!

Flo lay on her back in a bed of tall grass pressed flat by the tumult of two writhing bodies. Two bodies that a moment before had cleaved to each other in the explosive thrust of passion, but now lay apart, spent and exhausted. She thought of empty shotgun shells lying in a field after a dove shoot. She looked at the clouds drifting overhead, going who knows where. Something was troubling her about this man, this place. There was something odd. Perhaps it was just that the gulls had fallen silent, or . . . "Where's your car?" she asked lazily.

Adam sat bolt upright, all his senses suddenly alert. He had forgotten about the car! He saw it in his mind's eye on the main street of the small farming town where he had left it three days before with fifty cents in the meter. Too late now. He thought of the inevitable confrontation with the towing company, and he looked down at Flo's naked body in the grass beside him as if for the last time.

¶

IF WASHER FAILS TO START AFTER INSERTING QUARTERS, NOTIFY LANDLORD. DO NOT KICK IT!

¶

Fontini!

I was in my study working late last night when I was startled by the sound of breaking glass. I found on my living room floor what I presume to be your brick. This was, I suppose, a witty follow-up to your series of insulting postcards. (These I have turned over, along with the brick, to the police for analysis. Did you think of wearing gloves?) It is noble of you to want to avenge what you perceive as my insults to Mrs. Fontini, that cow. I suggest that having achieved whatever emotional solace one gets from hurling masonry, you now desist from further mischief.

Watchfully yours,
Whittaker

p.s. Where's my money?

¶

Dear Jolie,

Well, after spending I don't know how many hours last week staring at the photographs from Mama's box, I have found him (me) at last, thanks to a transparent plastic grid I rescued from your art supply satchel before I tossed it out (you should have sent me that list). I placed the photos one at time on the kitchen table. I laid the grid on top and scrutinized each photo through a magnifying glass, one square at a time, using the grid as guide. This is the technique the police use when they search a house for something very small, a minute fragment of bone from the victim, for example. They lay an imaginary grid over the whole house, and then they search the squares one after another. You have to check off each square as soon as you have looked in it, and you keep doing this until there are no squares left.

You can see how in the case of the photographs this was the way to go. Unless I had been sent away someplace (and wouldn't I remember that?), I surely must have blundered into at least one or two of the hundreds of snapshots: a clumsy, not-very-observant boy lumbering after a ball, perhaps, or tumbling down the steps ahead of an outsized father brandishing a belt, to explode into the viewfinder just as the shutter flew open. Of course they would have made a mental note to destroy that picture when it came back from the developer, but, I asked myself, would they always have remembered? How important, I reasoned, could my absence have been to them? Somewhere along the way, might they not have let a small fragment of bone slip into a crack? Perhaps they failed to notice me lurking in the distant background, maybe even hiding there.

So I sat myself at the kitchen table, all the photos in a big box on a chair beside me, and I scrutinized them one at a time, centimeter by centimeter, occasionally using a pair of calipers constructed from two pencils and a rubber band to gauge relative size and distance. After scanning each photo I marked it with a big D for "Done," though that could also stand for "Devoid of me" or even "Dud." My efforts, in the end, were not in vain. I was able to discover myself not once but three times: first as a vase, then as a dog, and finally as a strange boy peering from behind an obese woman. You laugh. I mean for you to laugh, though I am not joking.

Exhibit One. This is a snapshot of Peg, age about twelve, in shorts and halter. She is directing a jet of water from a garden hose against the side of a large black vehicle parked in

the driveway. I think it is a 1938 LaSalle. The water is ricocheting from the car into her face. Judging by her smile, she
seems not to mind this, and that fact, plus the shorts and halter, tells me the weather is very warm. A house, which I suppose is the house we lived in at the time, looms behind her,
two stories, unremarkable. We lived in so many houses,
moved so frequently, that I have only a jumble of architec-
tural fragments as memory of them, a door here, a water-
stained ceiling there. As for the house in the photograph, I
notice white curtains on the windows downstairs; on the
windows upstairs there are canvas shades. One shade has
been drawn all the way down. Perhaps someone is asleep in
that room, even though the little shadow puddled at Peg's
feet tells us it is the middle of the day. Perhaps the person in
that room has a hangover. Now look closely, as I did, and you
will see what appears to be an oviform vase sitting on the
interior sill of the window adjacent to that one. There is a
wire screen on that window and this, combined with the
smallness of the photo, makes it impossible to resolve the
image into a shape which will be entirely unambiguous.
There are stalks of things that appear to be flowers project-
ing from its top. I looked at it through the loupe. I scratched
my chin and then my nose, foraging for a clue, and then it
came to me: Why did I *assume* the egg-shaped thing was a
vase? Why couldn't it just as well be a head? Why *shouldn't* it
be? The longer I spent studying the picture, the more
intensely I could *feel* myself pressing my nose to the wire
screen as I tried to peer down from the window of my stifling
little closet of a room at Peg having fun with the hose.

I know what you are thinking, because I know how your
mind works when it comes to my ideas. You are going to say,

"What about the flowers? You *said* there seem to be flowers in that vase-like object in the window. I suppose you had flowers sprouting out of your head. Ha ha."

To this I respond: Why do you say those are flowers and not, say, feathers? For the nonce, instead of flowers, why not imagine an Indian headdress—how would *that* look? I don't remember owning one of those, but I don't remember *not* owning one either. In fact, I said those stalk-like things looked like flowers only because one *expects* flowers in a *vase;* but if it is a *head*, then they look like feathers. And *if* they look like feathers, then that thing is a head, a forlorn little head with its nose pressed to the screen.

Exhibit Two. Once again a car stands at the center. This time it's a station wagon of a make I can't identify. Papa and some man I don't recognize are standing behind the car. Each is holding a large fish by the gills, holding it high for the camera. Both are smiling, though the fish the other man holds is definitely larger than Papa's. I try to see whether Papa minds, but the photo is too small. I do, however, notice that the other man is holding his fish a little higher than Papa, which, considering his fish is heavier, might mean that he is prouder, or maybe just that he is stronger. At this period Papa was probably not very strong. He looks overweight and flabby. There are bags under his eyes, as if he were having difficulty sleeping, as he did later on after the psoriasis got out of control. You can see a lake on the other side of the car. At first glance, mesmerized by the fish, a casual viewer probably would not notice much else. But if he continues to look, as I did, especially if he uses a magnifier and applies the grid principle, he will eventually notice that something—or someone—is in the back seat of the station wagon. It looks at first glance like a large spaniel. Since we owned a series of springers, this interpretation cannot be ruled out with absolute certainty. On the other hand, it could just as well be the head of a boy wearing one of those hats with fur-lined ear flaps, with the flaps untied and hanging down. Once again, the mere fact that I don't remember such a hat cannot be used to exclude it, since I don't remember much of anything. If everything we do not remember did not exist, where would we be? Of course it seems to be a rather hot day for a fur hat, but maybe I was already self-conscious about my head being perhaps a trifle too small. Besides, why would a dog be sitting inside the car on such an obviously pleasant day? Is the dog angry because it didn't catch a fish? Does it sulk? Does it have tantrums?

Exhibit Three. This photo does not at first seem to be of anyone I know. For a third time a car occupies center stage, now locked in tight embrace with a panel truck. The photo shows the aftermath of a collision between a dark four-door sedan and a mid-sized delivery vehicle. The sedan has got the worst of it, grill and right fender hideously crushed. A policeman is leaning in at the window of the sedan, apparently talking to a person seated behind the steering wheel, though that person is concealed from us by the glare of the sun on the windshield. A sizeable crowd has gathered on the sidewalk across the street in front of a small store; I can tell it's a store by the Coca-Cola sign above the door. At first glance the crowd seems to be composed only of grown-ups. I do not, however, let myself become discouraged by this impression, and I continue to work my way step by step across the grid: yes, that really is a shoe, that really is a hat, that really is an elbow. And that, oh yes, *that* is a very small face. It is peering out from behind the voluminous skirt of an enormously obese woman. It is the face of a boy with blond hair, a furtive boy with blond hair who evidently does not *want* to be in the picture, or else he would not be hiding behind the fat woman's skirt; he would be out gawking with the rest of the folks. I know *I* would be out gawking, unless . . . And of a sudden the curtain rises, the entire scene shifts and becomes an altogether different scene, as in those drawings where a rabbit morphs precipitously into a duck for no other reason than that someone has remarked, "That's a duck." In similar fashion, the moment I said to myself, "That is *not* a picture of a traffic accident," the car and the truck fell away, became just incidental clutter in the foreground, while the face of the boy—now more frightened than furtive—lurched into prominence at the exact center of the photo, leaped forth, so to speak, as the true subject of the picture. Clearly this photo was someone's attempt to establish documentary proof (for Mama? for the Truant Officer?) that the boy was not where he was supposed to be (in school? at the dentist?). I tremble with excitement, I close my eyes, and Peg's little face, squinting from behind her box camera, floats into view. And there she is crawling under the house, where I am curled in the dirt next to the chimney, and if she gets any closer I am going to kick her.

Apart from my detective work, things here are not shaping up. My novel, which was meant to be comic, is not turning out as I envisaged. It has acquired an overlay of desperation which I doubt readers will find funny. And I spend too much time not doing anything. I sold the television last week. I don't turn on any lights unless I really have to. I find I can do most things in the dark, and I seldom read or write after sunset. I would like to say, "I sit in the dark and ponder," but I don't; I sit in the dark and fret. The rest of the time I sit in the blue and fret. I don't know how things have arrived at this sorry pass. (I say that, and I see the "things" struggling up a narrow trail in the high mountains toward a pass that is already blocked by snow.) Which decision was the wrong one? Or were there five wrong ones, or a thousand? People like to say that each moment presents us with a fork on our life path: I sit at my desk instead of going to the window, where perhaps I would have been hit by a brick, or going for a walk in the park, where I would have met a beautiful woman, a mugger, a man selling insurance, or no one at all; walking to the store, I turn on this street rather than that street; and everything is different forever. Have you ever wondered if the same thing might be true in the *other* direction? Going backwards, there are also choices to be made every step of the way, each item revived in memory only the first link of a new mnemonic chain, and every new chain recreating a different past, constructing a different album of photos, unpacking another box of forgotten treasures—a different past, which must of necessity be the past of a different present, a different future, a different *person*. The floor seems to drop away beneath us. A thousand personalities crowd onto our little stage. I see now that I can say *anything I want*.

I find myself crying about Mama.

I fret about the literary festival. I foresee a complete bust. I seem to make enemies right and left. Meanwhile the house grows increasingly unmanageable. I had put almost everything up in boxes, but then I had to take it all out again. Now I am trying to put it back in again. I feel overwhelmed by disorder. I don't know where it's coming from.

Beneath the sills? Through the cracks in the floorboards? Out of the light fixtures? The heat vents? It feels like an invasion of devouring ants. I open my mouth and they swarm out of it all over my shirt.

Love,

Andy

¶

Dear Dahlberg,

Doing those kind of things to your body is not going to make you a writer. NO ONE wants to hear about them. You MUST find someone to help you. But I am not that person. While I wish you happiness and good fortune, I am not going to open any letters you send in the future. Don't waste your time as they will fly straight into the trash can.

Andy

¶

To the Editor:

I read with interest the stimulating letter from Dr. Hawktiter on the subject of Andrew Whittaker, in which he points out how fortunate we are to have a writer of Mr. Whittaker's caliber in our midst. That is certainly the case. And it is true even for those of us who are not aware that he is here, for there is something to be said for living in a cultured community even if one does not partake of it personally, choosing TV over the stimulus of a good book. That is their right. However, I am not concerned here with Whittaker the controversial author. Let others judge his literary merits. Let others criticize if they dare his courageous support of struggling artists. No, I am concerned not with Andrew Whittaker, but with Andy, the man who lives across the street.

Six years ago an automobile accident snuffed out the lives of my husband Rob and my infant daughter Clarissa Jane and left me paralyzed from the waist down, confined to a wheelchair. One doesn't know how one goes on living after a tragic event like that, but somehow one does. And one can, thanks to small things like bird songs and game shows, and, let me add, thanks to big-hearted people like Andy. The day I came home from the hospital, he was there, a stack of books in his arms. I remember his gentle smile and the moisture in his eyes when he looked at my face, which was terribly mutilated. It was Andy who that very afternoon went through the closets and drawers and carried away all Rob's suits and shirts so I would never have to face those reminders of happier days.

How many times over the years since have I heard the merry jingle of the doorbell announcing one of his impromptu visits? He always does the shave-and-a-haircut thing on the bell. I laugh to think of it. Such a boyish thing to do, and yet so endearing. He possesses, how shall I put it? a spiritual bounciness that is totally contagious. After his visits I would find myself scooting about the house in my chair until the battery was quite dead. And my attendants love him too, especially the young girls, to whom he shows an old-world courtesy, though even the old ones are cajoled into allowing an occasional peck on the cheek. Dear old Andy. One day he comes with a loaf of raisin bread that he has baked himself, another day it's a single flower plucked from the park or an autumnal leaf that has caught his eye and that he hopes will bring me a little pleasure, light a match, as it were, in the dark corridor of my days. At other times, particularly on rainy days when there is nothing to be seen out the window, he will read to me from the classics, his sonorous voice wafting from room to room as he strides about the house in dramatic renditions of Ahab or Blind Pew or Count Dracula. He sometimes frightens the young attendants with these performances. We hardly know our gentle friend. But of course it's all in fun, and eventually they come back inside.

And then there are the marvelous meals he drops off in foil-covered plates, complete with a glass of either *rouge* or *blanc* as the dish may require. He has a discerning palate, though perhaps a bit overbearing when it comes to Indian spices. But this is so much his character that I never say anything, preferring just to do my best and drink a lot of water. Sometimes he stops by just for a little chat, and once when I had swallowed an eraser he saved my life. One of my great regrets is that I had no other children besides Clarissa Jane (and of course now it's too late). Such a pleasure it would have given them to have "Uncle Andy" drop by for a romp on the rug. As it is, my little dog Charlie is crazy about him as are all my nieces and nephews, though they rarely visit now. Their mother still blames me for Rob's death, though it was his idea for me to drive. And I was in a lot better shape than he was. Only my cats remain standoffish with Andy. Perhaps this is not because they don't like him but because they really do, and they sense that he is allergic to them. Poor Andy, he is allergic to so many things, not just cats and trees and flowers, but even to something like Pledge furniture polish which most people consider innocuous despite the warning on the label. You would be amazed at how many people use Pledge.

Andy says he feels completely surrounded by it. Many a time I have looked out my window (I often sit at my window) and have seen Andy in one of Rob's suits, worn now and shiny at the knees, leaning against a telephone pole, his nose streaming, while he struggles to catch his breath. And this is the man certain people would harry from pillar to post! I think we should all join Dr. Hawktiter in saying down with that!

Sincerely,

Dyna Wreathkit

❡

TO ALL TENANTS: MANAGEMENT HAS RECEIVED NOTICE FROM THE FIRE MARSHAL CONCERNING BICYCLES, STROLLERS, AND TOYS IN THE HALLS. THESE ITEMS ARE HAZARDOUS IN HALLS AND NEAR STAIRWAYS AND MUST BE KEPT IN YOUR APARTMENTS OR IN THE BASEMENT AT ALL TIMES. ITEMS FOUND IN VIOLATION WILL BE TRANSPORTED TO THE SALVATION ARMY.

THE MANAGEMENT

❡

Dear Mr. Freewinder,

There is really no need for apologies. I understand perfectly that your first duty is to American Midlands, and well it should be, for I dare say there is no finer bank of its size anywhere, especially now that you have that big new sign. I think making it out of bricks was a grand idea. Bricks, especially stacked several rows thick like that, convey a feeling of solidity, which the people who have entrusted their savings to you must find comforting indeed. I can't imagine how a sign made of wood—I am thinking of the plywood trifle they have over at First National—could reassure to the same degree. I wonder if the story of the three pigs had any influence on your decision to go brick. If it did, then you will probably think, when you read what I have to say, that I am like the foolish pig who built his house out of straw. If this turns out to be the case—and that will be for you to judge—then Whittaker Company might be so fragile at this time that it would be cruel and unwise of the bank to puff on it—unwise, because if it falls down, you will be left, to use a popular expression, holding the bag; and cruel, because there is someone inside. Inside and hard at work, and not, despite what you have been told, "cutting corners" in order to go "gadding about."

In better times I would have had my secretary scurry right over with the document you requested. Unfortunately, she has taken a powder, as the saying goes. To New York City, where she has ambitions of becoming an actress. That is not my fault, and I, personally, lay the blame on the movie magazines she found at her hairdresser. What do you think? As for the document, I must reluctantly report that I have not been able to find it in the mess. And now I would like to take a moment to say a word about that, about the mess.

It has been accumulating gradually, even relentlessly, a little each day since she bolted. Two years and sixteen days. Do you have any idea how long that is? To get an idea of the scope of it you have only to look at my desk. It is piled so high with "stuff" that I am not able to use it as a desk anymore. When there is something I must write, I am forced to stand and hold the paper up against a wall. In order to maintain some order I have tried from the outset to prevent the stacks from repeatedly sliding off onto the floor by applying bits of tape. This has been only partially successful and has had the drawback that when a stack finally does go, it goes all at once. Being held together with tape, it topples right over like a felled tree rather than just losing a portion off its top, its crown, as it were, as would otherwise be the case and as sometimes happens to trees in storms, especially pine trees. The presence of the tape also means that I cannot just peek into the middle of a stack and see what is in there. I would first have to dismantle the whole tower, and that, because of the tape, cannot be done without tearing. Some of the stacks have become so tall that I don't see how the dismantling, if I decide to go that route, can be achieved without creating an even bigger mess, the avoidance of which was, after all, the point of taping in the first place.

Of course if I knew for certain that your document was inside one of the stacks, I would have no qualms about just going at them a stack at a time, hacking and tearing my way through until I found it. But that is not the case. And just imagine how bad we both would feel if, at the end of it, I came up empty-handed. For we are not talking here about just a few thousand loose papers strewn across the floor; we are talking about thousands of loose papers with bits of sticky tape attached to them. Just picture people, perhaps children, desperate to get to the bathroom, having to cross over all that, the soles of their shoes picking up paper after paper. And though none of these papers may turn out to be the document you want, they are still important papers, poems and pieces of short stories and book reviews and the like, over which creative writers have sweated blood or worse, even if they, the papers, are, as of course they will be by that time, crumpled and sticky. And what do you think those people, now thoroughly irked and exasperated, are going to do with these important papers once they are in the bathroom with the door locked? I know you will agree that before letting this happen we have an obligation to dig to the bottom of every other possible hiding place, no matter how dubious or remote.

The filing cabinets, for example. Five sturdy steel ones. Together they contain seventeen drawers, if we still count as "drawer" one which has lost its front part or "facing" (the part that had the handle), and which is now a kind of sliding tray. I suppose, in the case of this one, "ex-drawer" might be better than "drawer," in which case the sum of genuine drawers drops to sixteen.

Currently, from my present position in the room, leaning a shoulder against a wall next to the door, I am able to survey all five cabinets, and it strikes me that, if we take the word "contain" in its strict and proper sense, then they in fact contain only twelve drawers, since four of the drawers are so overfilled with *stuff* it is impossible to push them shut, and in that condition, hanging out over the floor like that, they cannot, without a laxity of speech which in my view we ought to avoid, be described as *contained*.

Earlier this year, when my health permitted exertions of that stripe, I endeavored to force those drawers back in with my feet. By kicking, of course, which was completely ineffective, but also by lying supine on the floor, knees bent, and pushing with the flat of my feet against the front of the drawer. The outcome was not as I had hoped. When I straightened my knees and shoved, my whole body slid, indeed shot, across the linoleum floor in the opposite direction. I tried this with all four drawers, and in every case the same thing happened, and in no case did a drawer budge so much as an inch. I did succeed, however, in bending in the front part or "facing" of all four drawers and flattening the silver-metal pull handle tightly against it. Now, on further reflection, this—the fact that the drawers did not slide in—seems to me a fortunate accident. Had I succeeded in forcing them shut with my feet, I can't imagine how, without handles, I could ever have opened them again, in which case your document, if it is in one of them, would be irretrievable.

Yet even as things stand and by virtue of no footwork on my part, the cabinets already contain three drawers firmly stuck in the "in" or "shut" position. In fact they have been stuck in that position since before she bolted, a period when I was not "in charge." I really ought to have subtracted those three from the drawer list at the outset, since, functionally speaking, they are ex-drawers. Making this belated correction, we find the total number of genuine drawers actually contained has shrunk to nine, which probably sounds like a manageable number to you, as it did to me when I first arrived at it yesterday morning. I was lying on the sofa after a sleepless night, listening to the first birds calling plaintively from somewhere. Despite exhaustion, my initial impulse on finally reaching this number was to jump right in, just spring up from the sofa and excavate those nine drawers, one drawer at a time, one sheet of paper at a time. But scarcely had I swung my feet to the floor and planted them firmly there (resolved, as I said, to dig in), than it dawned upon me that in my enthusiasm at getting there at last I was about to behave in a manner which was anything but rational. You see, *I had nothing to go on*—nothing, that is, more substantial than a wild hope that the document was, somehow, somewhere, in one of the nine. Yet for me actually to *know* that this was the case—and not merely an illusion born of wishful thinking—would necessitate hours, even days, of tedious labor carried out from an uncomfortable posture. And at the end of it all, should I choose to go that route, I might still come up empty-handed, since it is possible, even plausible, that the document is not in any of the drawers that are accessible to me but in one of the three that are presently stuck hopelessly shut or even, as I said before, in one of the stacks on the desk. And if that is the case, as now seems likely, then all those hours, even days, on my knees, practically up to my hips in waste paper, would be just precious time squandered. In short, I considered it crucial at that point in my enquiry, even before I started looking *anywhere*, to make certain that I could look *everywhere*, including in the stuck drawers. Then, though I might still not find your document, I could in good conscience at least write you a letter beginning, "After an exhaustive search, I regret . . ."

You will note that this is not how I began this letter, and with reason. After working step by step through the reflections I have sketched above, I felt that out of deference to you I had no choice but to try and get the stuck drawers open, pry them out by main force should that prove necessary. Yet just as I was working the blade of a large screwdriver into the crack between one of the drawers and the frame of the cabinet, and was preparing to lean heavily upon it, I lost it down an air vent, lost the screwdriver down there. It flew out of my hand, did a kind of double somersault in the air, and dove straight through the grillwork of the vent. If I lie on the floor and put my eye to the vent, I can see it on a little ledge about two feet down into the duct, but I can't reach it. I have tried a coat hanger, but only managed with that to move it into a more precarious position at the rim of the ledge, with all of its handle and a portion of its shank hanging out over what seems to be a bottomless drop. Another quarter inch and it's gone. I thought of removing the grill that covers the vent in order to be able to reach in with my arm, only to discover that it, the grill, is fastened down with screws.

All this is very distressing, and to make matters worse I have syncopes. I am, fortunately, usually warned of an impending attack by seeing spots, dark fuzzy disks floating across my vision. This is an eerie sensation; the spots seem to flit in the air a foot or two in front of my face, and I feel I could, if I wanted, reach out and snag one. I imagine, were this possible, that it would feel like something furry in my hand. The moment I see the spots, I try to situate myself near a soft receptacle of some sort, a sofa for example, or if I am in the street, I step into the flower beds, if there are any. If there are not, I sit down on the pavement. But sometimes the syncopes come without warning when I am walking past my desk, and then, as I go down, I drag piles of stuff with me onto the floor. This is part of the reason there is such a mess down there now. I had not mentioned the floor part, the incredible mess there, before, for fear of appearing discouraged at the outset, and of giving you the impression that I was not even trying. I have a dreadful inkling that your document is down there somewhere, though the syncopes make it difficult for me to be certain, since whenever I bend down to take a look, I get spots. Instead of auditors, I think you would do better to send one or two of your girls over to help me clean up. Also, if they could bring some large plastic bags with them, for the stuff we don't want, and a screwdriver.

Dear Mr. Freewinder, I have now been leaning my elbows against a wall for over forty minutes. In order to make my pen write in this position I have had to pause every dozen or so words and shake it violently. And yet, with all that, I have not addressed your central question, about the financial "viability" of the business. You are wondering if it is going bust. I sympathize with your concern, and I would have answered with a firm Yes or No at the outset, to spare you anxiety, had I been able, but the truth is, I haven't the foggiest. And this is really the point I have been trying to drive home all along, the reason I went on about the mess, the syncopes, and so forth, in the first place, "carrying on," as it must seem to you, about things which are not terribly interesting and which you might consider depressing. Are you aware that I publish a literary magazine that is read all over the country, a magazine that makes enormous demands on my time? Are you aware that, on top of this, I have a literary vocation of my own and better things to do with my waking hours than rack rents and unplug toilets? Probably not. Ever since she bolted, I have been forced by circumstances to adopt the most primitive—yet, for that very reason, the most tried and true—business practice short of the abacus. When money comes in, I put it in a jar. It is a large jar of clear glass, so it can hold a lot, should that ever happen, and I can see at a glance how much is in there. The mail arrives each day. If there is a bill, I look in the jar to see if I can pay it. If I can, I do. If I can't, I put it on the desk. In order to maintain some semblance of fairness—the old idea of "first come, first served"—I try to work it in at the bottom of one of the stacks, with the help of a table knife. I also sometimes take money out of the jar in order to buy things for myself—food and items of personal hygiene. However, I am scrupulous on this point: I always replace the extracted funds with a corresponding slip of paper bearing the exact amount extracted and the date. So, to return to your question as to whether Whittaker Company is broke, or not broke, the best I can do is report what I presently see in the jar: several greenbacks, at least one of which is a fiver, and a great many paper slips.

In closing, let me say that I am pleased that American Midlands still thinks of us as partners. I, likewise, am always ready to work with *you* in order to move forward together.

Sincerely,

Andrew Whittaker

¶

Dear Dahlberg,

I can't imagine what a meeting between us would accomplish. You have already heard everything I have to say. You complain about no vacation time and no money, so WHAT IS THE POINT of a long trip like that? We have absolutely no room here, so you would have to pay for a hotel.

Andy

¶

Dear Fern,

Even though I knew Mr. Crawford had been, as you have said repeatedly, a "huge figure" in your life, I was not prepared for this. I just assumed you had asked a girlfriend from school to hold the camera. I still can't fathom why you would find that "horribly embarrassing," while asking your old English teacher to do the same thing is not. Nor do I grasp what you mean by saying he was the "logical" person to ask because "he was in on the ground floor anyway."

I don't want to sound unsympathetic. I know it must be much more relaxing for you not to have to worry about the self-timer—after all, I was the one who spotted the problem. As to the presence of Mr. Crawford, being something of an amateur clown myself—did I ever tell you that?—I know how stimulating a live audience can be, no matter how meager or aged. After all, what good are antics if there is no one around to laugh? Of course, I don't mean to suggest that Mr. Crawford was laughing. On the contrary, what *was* he doing? No sooner do I ask this than I am besieged by swarms of mental pictures, which I am doing my best to swat. Even though he was in on the ground floor and knows all about cameras, are you sure he is the best person for this? How *old* is he?

Plans for the festival are roaring on. It swells apace even as we speak. Here at the office we shade our eyes and gaze ahead; it balloons before us. Though knocked to the floor by the bulges of its massiveness, we wrestle with it. We have set up committees to control its aspects and appendages. Do you think bumper cars would be *de trop?* I thought we could give the cars the names of literary fashions—Romanticism, Realism, etc.—and a person could choose his affiliation and crash it into the others. Have you read Rimbaud?

There will be a parade on the final day featuring huge papier-mâché puppets representing the great authors. We'll have the local schoolchildren make them in art class (I expect to enlist the whole community in some aspect of this gigantic effort). In addition to the lecture series and the rides, there will be elephants. And a parade, of course. You have no idea how much it costs to rent even one elephant, and to feed it while you have it, so we can't leave them just standing around eating. The parade's pinnacle, the *pièce de résistance*, coming I think about midway along in the procession, will be a magnificent flower-encrusted float bearing a beautiful woman reclining on a gigantic plywood replica of an open book. The book's title will be clearly visible—*A Thousand and One Nights*—set in flashing colored lights. That way even the semiliterates and country people from miles around, who will have been attracted in droves by rumors of elephants, will recognize Scheherazade, literature's own concubine, mistress and muse of storytellers, diaphanous in Persian silks. She will be the same woman whom the night before I will have named "Miss Soap" to the deafening applause of assembled dignitaries on the State House steps. Whenever I think of this eventual person the photograph of you in that garment soars into my mind and sticks there like a wet leaf. And your being an author makes it doubly perfect. Would you consent? Naturally the festival will cover all your expenses including wardrobe (or lack thereof—ha ha) and meals. The schedule is tight, the pace frenzied, the days (I hope) will be sunny. I must have your answer soon.

Andy

¶

socks
checks
copy keys
different kind deli meat
next 5 days
t.p.
sponge
vodka mix
what else

¶

Dahlberg,

I FORBID you to come. The mere fact that we do not agree on artistic matters does not mean that I need "straightening out." What do you mean by that anyway? I am a sick man. I cannot have house guests. Forget it.

Andy

¶

Dear Jolie,

My last letter to you was filled with warm feelings, and in reply I get that photograph—an interesting lesson in the art of backstabbing. However, you seem to have forgotten that I have grown thick calluses over my most vulnerable organ. Thanks to this innovation your blade failed to penetrate it, though I bled. Have you also forgotten your reaction a few years back when you saw the picture in the paper of Quiller on his motorcycle? To refresh your memory: there was a mouse-faced leather-clad Lolita clinging like a monkey-child to his back, and the photo bore the caption "Best Selling Novelist at Full Throttle." I think I sneered. I think you said, "Poor Marcus, how embarrassing." And then you chuckled. And now it's *you*. By right it should be my turn to shake the chuckle box, but I've lost the knack, or the taste. Why do you tell me *now* how great you feel in leather? What am I supposed to do with this information? What am I suppose to do with this photograph? Show it around? "And here's my ex on a Harley-Davidson motorcycle with the famous Pulitzer-hunting ass-kissing poseur Marcus Quiller?" You are not eighteen. Do you have any idea how ridiculous you look? Is your purpose to torment me? By doing that do you suppose I will feel encouraged to buckle down and "do something" about the properties as you suggest? I *am* doing something about them, and it doesn't work. Instead of hauling in the dough, I am crawling around the house on all fours, afraid to stand up for fear of heavy objects arriving rapidly through a window. There is also an oversexed female with a blowtorch on the loose, not to mention her husband the poison toad. I am trying to keep my head up. No, I am trying to keep my head down. The nights are getting colder. How am I to pay to heat this place when winter comes?

As you gather from the above, there is a certain iffyness to my life these days, as in "If I put a bullet through my brain will I regret it later?" The house feels more and more like a lonely place. I think those people are fantastically lucky who live in houses where they can call out and expect someone to answer. I have started eating with my fingers because I can't stand the clinking of the cutlery against the plate. It is too evocative of someone eating by himself.

I am not having hysterics, and how dare you call my ants histrionic?

Andy

¶

Pistol to the temple
Pistol in the mouth
Pistol to the heart
Pistol to the foot
Pistol to the foot plus sepsis
Hanging, drowning
Lysol

¶

SAFE AND AFFORDABLE! 2711 General Sherman Highway. 1 bdrm unit in brick bldg. Partly furnished. New paint. Heat incl. Soft-drink dispenser in basement. 10-min to dog track, 15-min to Johnson Sheet and Girder. No pets, no loudmouths. $110

¶

Dear Harold,

So glad you like my dictionary of pain idea. I, likewise, am intrigued by *your* idea for an appendix on pronouncing animal sounds, and especially your suggestions of ways to transcribe their cries. When you say you have been turning these over in your mind as you go about your chores, I picture you emitting all sorts of hoots, howls, and whistles, while you bounce over the furrows with troops of excited animals running behind. As you point out, some of the cries are almost human. I hadn't realized that farm life was so gruesome, and I'm sorry about your little boy.

Which reminds me of a funny story I almost told you in my last letter, about pain and how we express it or not. It ties in with the rough times you said you and Catherine had at the outset. It is actually two stories, or one story with two parts, and only the second part is funny.

Jolie and I had been married for less than two years when her stepfather died and left us some money, though it was not the amount we expected. We had fallen into the habit, just as a joke, of referring to it as a pile, as in "Wait till we get John's pile," and after a while we believed it. But in the end it was not a pile, and we spent the whole of it on half a summer in Paris instead of the full year we had planned. Jolie wanted very much to go to Rome, where her real father is buried (he was killed in the war), and I think it was my insistence on Paris that got her started. She is, despite a very pleasant exterior, at bottom a sullen creature capable of cold-hearted resentments. Though I was in love with her, I knew even then that she was not an attractive person in every respect. Her carping and backbiting on the boat going over—constantly pointing out that after all it was *her* money—had so worn me down by the time we reached Paris it was hardly surprising when I fell violently ill our first evening there, embarrassing us both by losing my supper on the Boulevard Saint-Germain. I was laid up in our little apartment for a good ten days after that.

Jolie, indefatigable tourist that she was, or appeared to be, did not let this alter her plans. And I agreed she shouldn't, though in fact I felt betrayed and abandoned. Every morning she would descend the five flights of narrow wooden stairs to the street for a coffee and croissant at a dingy little bistro on the corner, and return with a large bottle of Vichy water for me. Following the strict regimen endorsed by the *patronne* of the bistro (Jolie: "French people know *all* about this kind of thing"), I was supposed to sip the water at half-hour intervals throughout the day, plus a full glass with a boiled potato at meal times. After handing over the water, there would be a kiss of quick good-bye, and, Fodor's in hand, off she would trot on her adventures. Except for precipitous visits to the reeking WC in the hall, I stayed put all day, prisoner in our matchbox apartment, dozing or sitting miserably at the kitchen window gazing at the stupid pigeons on the rooftops across the street, waiting for evening and her return.

For the first few days, beguiled by her manner (the pleasant exterior I mentioned) and by the thought that of course I knew Jolie, I didn't suspect a thing. Arriving home in the late afternoon, chirpy as a wren, she would kick off her shoes—"absolutely bushed" from "traipsing" all over Paris— and sit on my bed, if I was in bed, or on the floor in the hall, her back against the WC door, if that's where I was, and talk to me about the places she had visited. How could I have guessed that she was pilfering the descriptions from the guidebook? True, when she kissed me good-bye on setting out each morning, it was on the forehead instead of on the lips as before; I noticed, but thought she was just avoiding my microbes. It was the smell that finally gave her away. My olfactory powers are normally quite muted—I have to stuff a rose up a nostril in order to smell it. Maybe the purging blandness of boiled potatoes and Vichy water had sharpened them, but the fact is it was a smell that betrayed her. Cheap

Paris hotels in those days didn't have bathtubs or even showers—I mean the sort of hotel a pair of economizing lovers might resort to for an afternoon—and Jolie, innocent that she was, had no idea what to do with a bidet. I was crawling under the sheet one morning looking for my socks when the truth was borne in upon me.

To make a long story short—in fact it was not very long; it only felt as if it were lasting forever—we ended up in a *ménage à trois* with young Gustav Lepp, a teacher at a secondary school near our apartment. (This is not the funny part.) Jolie had met him in the breakfast bistro on our second day in Paris. He was one of those people you can spend an evening with and be utterly charmed, swept off your feet by their wit, their erudition, the fact that they seem *extremely interested in you*, only to wake up next morning with the feeling that you've been had. Their affair lasted for seven weeks. Even now I can recall in excruciating detail, as if it were yesterday, listening as if transfixed to the gasps and cries from the bedroom, five feet from where I sat at the kitchen table staring at my face in my coffee. It was part of the ideology of the time that this sort of behavior was normal, even desirable, and to keep myself from wailing in agony I would stuff my mouth full of bread. When they would leave off at last and emerge glistening with sweat to join me in the kitchen, I would turn away to the sink as if to draw a glass of water, and there I would let the bread dribble quietly from my mouth, forcing it down the drain with a spoon, while they sat down at the table and spread jam on theirs. That's the reason I don't eat white bread now, on account of the memories that rush in the instant I taste it and make it impossible to swallow, only whole wheat or rye. Somehow we got through the summer, though it was thoroughly spoiled for me. And this, I suspect, was Jolie's aim all along, a way of pointing out that we ought to have gone to Rome, where none of this would have happened. When I wasn't tagging after the two of them, as a tiresome third, I would tail them at a distance in order to obsessively observe every kiss and caress. As a consequence I saw next to nothing of Paris—not the Louvre, not even Notre Dame. I must have passed near both places many times, but I could not *see* anything, blinded as I was by the visions that filled my mind. Our money mercifully ran out in August. After we had returned to the States they tried to keep up a correspondence, but this too petered out after a few months.

Years went by, and I was confident that I had left the worst of it behind me. Jolie and I were able to prepare beignets de courgettes together, enjoy French movies again, and even discuss them afterwards without shouting. Then one Sunday morning about five years ago Gustav Lepp turned up unannounced on our doorstep. I heard the thrill in Jolie's voice when she answered the bell, and without lifting my head from the morning paper I knew who it was. He had not changed, except to grow more so. More witty, more charming, more tanned, more vain, and, if this is possible, more tall. I, meanwhile, was looking increasingly like a ticket-taker in the Metro, right down to the little paunch, the bad teeth, and the ill-fitting pants. He had written a book, *On the Phenomenology of Lust*, and apparently was famous now in some psychotic niche of the university world. He was just stopping by on the way to a lectureship in California. So of course we invited him to stay for lunch. And it was not an unpleasant meal—we were after all practically middle-aged people by then. We discussed lust, of course, or rather he discussed it, while I kept an eye on their feet under the table.

After lunch I went to wash up as usual, since Jolie had cooked, while they took their coffee out back on the terrace. I had advised against that, since it seemed to me the air had turned chilly—it was October, after all—but they brushed me off with a laugh, Gustav Lepp shouting back something about *la chaleur d'amitié*. I thought I had put it all behind me, but to my surprise, to my *shock* really, I experienced at that instant such a rush of inexplicable rage that I was compelled to turn away to the sink, again! I plunged both hands deep in the soapy water and gripped tightly the rim of a large serving platter at the bottom. Though the water was painfully hot, I remained like that, head bowed, until the feeling had subsided and I could go about the business of tidying up. I had almost finished by the time Jolie came in, I hoped for good, though it was only to fetch the Sunday *Times* and blankets so they could stay on the terrace a while longer. She pressed me to join them, but I declined on the pretext that the fish tank needed cleaning.

The tank stood next to a window that gave on to the terrace, and as I knelt beside it and began scraping algae from the glass, I was amused to observe that I could make out their wavering shapes through the water. Side by side in deckchairs on the terrace, they appeared to be drowning among the angel fish and mollies. A heap of newspaper lay between them, from which each had taken a favorite section: Jolie the Arts and Leisure, and Gustav Lepp the Week in Review. I watched them turn the pages, bringing their arms to their chests and then flinging them out, and I thought of butterflies slowly beating their wings as they drowned. I watched, fascinated, as a large black snail crawled in the direction of Gustav Lepp's (I now noticed) slightly balding head.

Soon afterwards I heard the animated murmur of renewed conversation. Leaving the fish—I had nearly finished, and it was anyway supposed to be Jolie's chore—I slipped out the front door, and going around by the driveway, still wet from an afternoon shower, tiptoed up on the terrace. I held in my hand a straight pin I had picked up from the floor the day before and placed on the mantel, where I happened to catch sight of it on my way out. As I drew near the terrace, I realized I could just as well have kept my shoes on; they were absorbed in conversation— Jolie's plans for her life now that she had decided to become a painter—and oblivious of my approach. I had been right about the cold and, *en plus*, my socks were now soaking wet. Dropping to all fours (I almost wrote "like a panther"), I crawled across the flagstones until I was crouching directly behind Gustav Lepp's chair. He was telling Jolie, "It's important, I think, that one have a public visage, a way of defining oneself apart from one's husband and what really after all is *his* work. That is just common sense." At the conclusion of the word "sense" I reached up with my pin and gently pricked the back of his neck. I had meant it to be nothing more than a mosquito bite, so you can imagine my mirth when he reached back and slapped the spot. My second prick was rather more assertive. Jolie was talking— "Yes, I know, I've always felt a need for expression. During my first year at college . . ."—when she was interrupted by a Gallic cry of pain: "Aie!" She stopped in midsentence. "Gustav Lepp, what?" At this point I was not able to stifle my laughter, which burst through my closed lips, I regret rather laden with spittle. Gustav Lepp turned and peered over the back of his chair down at me where I crouched grinning and wiping my chin with my hand. He said, rather humorlessly, "I believe this is what you call playing the card." I later turned this phrase into something of a joke between Jolie and me. (This is the funny part.) She would come out with something she considered amusing, and I would say in my best French accent, "I believe zees is what you call playing zee card." In context this was often extremely droll, though it seemed to vex Jolie. Of course I never used it if what she had said was actually amusing, and my little intervention often saved the day, provoking smiles all around, where otherwise there would have been only embarrassment and blank looks.

Well, Harold, I have spent a long time telling you all this—my little Olivetti is fairly smoking—and now I wonder why I bothered. True, I had been thinking about pain, and in an earlier letter I talked about the way French speakers express it. The mind, I have found, is just one thing after another, especially lately, but that hardly justifies the intimacy of what I have just told you. Does it strike you as unseemly? I think I find it easy to talk to you because I don't remember you very well. It's like talking to the furniture, but with the added attraction that in your case the furniture understands, or at least pretends it does. Ever since you wrote I have tried to picture you. In the beginning, the chubby rubicund fellow I used to best every Saturday at ping-pong would come to mind, but of course I knew this could not be you still, so I have tried to update the image with the bits of information you have given me in your

letters, and I have ended up, vaguely I'm afraid, with someone in overalls.

Your old friend,
Andy

¶

Dahlberg,

You will find no one home. I am going to Italy for the
winter. I have something in my chest. If after beating your
fists blue on the door you decide to go around and peer
through the windows on the side, please take care while
crossing the flowerbeds, which I am in the process of reseed-
ing. Also, I have asked the police to keep an eye on the property, so you should try and not look suspicious.

Arrivederci,
Andrew

¶

Adam's knuckles were white, for he was gripping the steering wheel of the big pickup with a fury born of the knowledge that his car might even now be hanging from the hook
of a battered tow truck. Or perhaps it had already been
released, hitting the ground with a thud that had injured the
front shock absorbers or the delicate torsion bars. Anything,
he knew, was possible. They could have left it in gear during
the towing and damaged the automatic transmission, dam-
age that might not show up for years. He thought of all the
precision-milled gears, the tiny valves, the fragile gaskets,
intricate clutches and torque converters that must work

together in a smoothly shifting automatic transmission of European manufacture, and he shuddered. Flo, sitting close beside him, laid off tugging at the shreds of her blouse and looked up. She saw the clenched jaw and the white knuckles and the reckless skill with which he handled the big truck on the narrow blacktop, and she wondered at the source of the violence which seemed to animate his every gesture. After all, she had given herself to him willingly, as she had to most men who gave her half a chance—in cars, on the gravel in the back of filling stations, in tents, barns, toilet stalls, phone booths, even once in a Ford Torino with two police officers—and yet he had insisted on ripping her clothes off, including her underpants, which were so damaged she had had to leave them in the grass in front of the shack, and the embroidered blouse with puff sleeves, which she now held closed with one hand, while with the other she caressed Adam's right thigh even as he held his foot firmly on the accelerator. Violence, but also a quiet bitterness. She dimly sensed that whatever dark forces were driving him had their roots in a past which was still closed to her. She was wondering if perhaps he had suffered abuse at the hands of a close relative while still a child, when they came to an intersection. "Turn left here," she shouted. Braking for the turn, he reached for the floor shift. "Excuse me," he muttered, as he fumbled between her thighs in search of the shift lever. Finding it, he shifted smoothly into second, and then, as the big truck regained speed, he dragged the stick back down into third, before resuming his knuckled grip on the wheel, while Flo closed her thighs once again on the vibrating knob of the shifter. She looked over at the strong thick-veined hands and the rows of white knuckles on the steering wheel, and she thought of the miniature eggs the chickens had laid after they got sick, when they laid any eggs at all, which most of them couldn't. Of course, even when they could, they laid them higgledy-piggledy wherever they happened to be when the urge hit them and never in neat rows of four like Adam's knuckles.

Now she was beset by a new apprehension. She twisted in her seat to look back at the John Deere riding mower on the trailer, for it was on a trailer in fact and not in the bed of the truck as before, skittering and fish-tailing behind them, and the sight of it made her shudder also. She knew that with the exception of his thirty-seven volume Almanac collection and her mother's hairbrush, in which a few last gray hairs were still tangled in wistful reminder, the big John Deere riding mower was her father's dearest possession. During the first terrible year after the accident visitors to the farm would usually find the once hale old farmer slumped dejectedly in an old rocker on the rotting front porch, perhaps lifting a wizened head to halloo intermittently for his daughter, who was invariably out of earshot milking in the cow shed or else in the hay with one of the many delivery men who were wont to stop by with increasing frequency as did salesmen of various useless articles and a deputy sheriff as well. Or else, getting no answer from her, he might be struggling in vain to drive his wheelchair through the deep sand in the yard, or, if it had rained the night before, he might already be sunk up to the axle there, pounding his fists on the chair arms and shouting for his daughter to fetch the pickup and snatch him out. As a consequence of being in this manner impaired and restricted, the proud old man, who had never had to ask a helping hand of anyone before, felt sorely diminished.

Sometimes he would say as much to his daughter as she knelt beside him tying a rope to his chair. "I feel sorely diminished, daughter" he would say, "and if I could find the fucker that hit me I'd blow his dick off and make him eat it, and after that I'd kill him."

Flo was troubled by the bitterness he was lately wont to spit forth from his mouth on many occasions, and she racked her brain for some way to make his life altogether more pleasant, and one day she hit on the idea of dragging the big mower out of the barn and gassing it up. From the moment it coughed to life in a vast display of white smoke and considerable backfiring, her father's days were not the same. There was, spiritually speaking, a new spring in his instep and, once he had got the phlegm up, a cheery ring to his voice when he hallooed for his breakfast at daybreak. After eggs and bacon or sausage, Flo would help him up on the mower. Once up, he could ride all day long, pausing only for lunch and a toilet break or to fill up with gas from the big red tank by the barn, and not dismount until the orb of the sun had turned blood-red in the west. Even blight-stricken and sorely weakened as they were, the surviving chickens had managed to eat every last blade of grass in the yard and most of the zinnias, so there was not much to mow there anymore. After a couple of weeks of spinning around in clouds of dust, the old man was sick and tired of it, so he mowed down the hollyhocks Flo's mother had planted next to the house and most of the shrubbery as well, though the mower finally got hung up on a big lilac bush by the porch, and Flo had to drag it off with the pickup. After they had ordered a new blade from town, and one of the salesman who had stopped by had helped them fit it, he took up mowing the grass shoulders of the county road that ran in front of the farm. This was supposed to be the county workers' job, for which they were paid handsomely, but by setting his blade lower than theirs would go he managed always to get the best of them. When they were not able to find anything high enough to make shorter, they would just stand around scratching and talking till lunchtime and then run their big mowers back up on the yellow trucks and leave. After a few months, when they saw they could count on the proud old farmer to keep things neat and trimmed, they stopped coming altogether. But the shoulders of the road, which he now mowed all the way to the outskirts of Parkersville, were not enough for the energetic old man, and he fell into the habit of turning into neighbors' farms and mowing everything he could find there. Sometimes the people were happy to have their grass cut for free, but sometimes they drove him off with spray from a garden hose or a rain of dirt clods.

Flo was remembering all this when she turned suddenly to look at the mower bounding behind them on the trailer, and she forgot that she did not have buttons anymore. The ripped shirt fell open and Adam noticed once again how closely her breasts resembled Glenda's. They could have been from the same woman, and for a moment he had the nightmarish conviction that they were. Flo noticed his sharp intake of breath as he struggled with this thought. For a moment he lost control of the vehicle. He regained it quickly, though, shooting a rooster tail of gravel across the shoulder as he powered out of the skid. The trailer hit the pavement again with a jolt that caused the mower to leap in the air, and when it landed back on the trailer it was with one wheel hanging off the side spinning. "We're gonna lose her," Flo shouted, but Adam paid no heed, for he was once more bar-reling grimly down a straight stretch, his jaw muscles work-ing. She wondered if he was chewing on something, perhaps a blade of grass he had picked up while they were locked in wild embrace in front of the shack or maybe afterwards when she was inside looking for a safety pin. She let her gaze slide in a slow caress from his jaw to his shoulder and noticed for the first time how thick his neck was. And now she won-dered once again at the audacity of her choice, as she had wondered before with other men, and boys too, her twin nephews for example, though not to the same degree.

Just at that moment the road made a wide turn to the left and Adam swept into it with no decrease in forward speed. Flo began to slide sideways across the seat, which was cov-ered in slippery blue plastic, for her father was not given to useless luxury in his pickups, and had declined to shell out for leather, or some soft fabric, despite the salesman's warn-ing that plastic would make his ass sweat like a pig on a spit. She instinctively grabbed at the gear lever around which her knee was hooked also. "Let go the damn shifter!" Adam shouted. It was the first time he had raised his voice to her since he had ordered her down on all fours back at the shack, and in her astonishment she let go the shifter. She shot across the seat and slammed up against the passenger door, where she was jabbed a sharp one in the ribs by the window crank. She let out a cry of pain. But Adam did not turn his head, and she remained slumped against the door, glowering darkly, a strand of damp hair falling across her face, until they reached the farm, for that is where they were going. Adam's rage, however, was soon tempered by bitter remorse, and he smiled wanly at her through his teeth. He was about to beg her forgiveness when suddenly she shouted, "Here it is, turn here." Adam jerked the big truck hard to the right into a narrow dirt drive that ran up to the farmhouse. At which point the John Deere mower became airborne again, this time in a mostly sideways direction, and flew into the large white-painted wooden sign announcing "Happy Daze Dairyfarm," which it proceeded to splinter. Fortunately this same turn also flung Flo back across the seat where she slammed up against Adam, and where they both again felt the surge of their first contact.

At the end of the long driveway bordered by the leafless stubble of boxwood hedges, they could see the stately old farmhouse, now sadly in need of sundry repairs, nestled under the two big oak trees. Adam inched the big truck forward, so the handful of chickens pecking in the gravel could stagger out of the way, some of them falling down when they tried to hurry and having to be helped up by the others. He noticed a few gumball-sized eggs scattered here and there in the sand, the hens having wandered off and forgotten about them as they were wont to do ever since they had contracted the blight.

Flo's father saw them approaching—heard them before he saw them due to the crash of the John Deere mower against the sign, though he did not know that that was what it was, thinking instead that one of the salesman had run into the ditch as they sometimes did in their eagerness—and he came down to meet them, using a gently sloping wooden ramp especially constructed for that purpose. Adam swung the big truck around and skidded to a stop with the driver's door just a few feet from the old man's wheelchair, causing the old farmer to vanish from sight for several minutes in the large cloud of dust that came rolling in behind them. This cloud and the fit of coughing and expectoration that ensued allowed Flo to slip out on the passenger side and streak into the house unseen, from which she emerged moments later clad in an attractive summer frock buttoned to the neck

"Adam Partridge?" the old man said as he clasped Adam's hand in a hardy grip. "Estelle Partridge's boy?" Adam nodded. He sat on a stump next to the old man's chair and laid out the situation.

"That'll be Stint Bros. Towing that's got your car, son," the old man said ominously. "Dahlberg Stint and his brother Tiresome." He spit in the dirt next to his chair, a phlegmy gob that caused a few hopeful chickens to stagger closer. Adam looked down at them tugging listlessly at the stringy mess, and his eye for the first time fell on the Winchester rifle in the leather scabbard hanging at the side of the wheelchair. He had assumed it was a large umbrella probably. The old man continued: "More than likely those boys have got her stripped down by now. Come Saturday your radio and tape player's gonna be on a table at the new flea market they got down Kenosha way. Hubcaps too probably. Young fellows around here think mighty highly of those Mercedes caps. Bend the flanges a little and make 'em fit a Chevy." Adam drew nearer, and Flo, who was on the porch shelling peas, could not catch more than a word or two now and then. She listened to the quiet susurration of their mutters, and smiled when a hearty laugh or bitter imprecation reached her ears. She occasionally lifted her gaze from the peas to watch them: her father, wizened and calm and stoical in his suffering, and this young man, mercurial and strangely tormented. So different, and yet . . . She noticed the angle of the jaws, the long straight noses, the cleft chins, and the odd combination of delicate facial features and thick necks. Adam had also noticed this, and he had noticed too the catch in the old man's voice when he had pronounced the name Estelle Partridge, pronounced it aloud for the first time in thirty-three years. At that moment he could not help but wonder if it was really just warm Coke that had caused his parents to suddenly abandon their ancestral plot and move to California, or was it something darker? And Flo on the porch was wondering the same thing, for Adam had told her the whole story when they were lying in the grass. Suddenly the aged oaks behind them seemed to loom menacingly, like large beasts standing on their hind legs ready to fall upon them with all the weight of the past. They shivered, Adam and Flo shivered, and yet at the same time they rejoiced, feeling the hot pull of blood to blood. And beneath the rearing oaks they silently called to each other across the chicken yard.

In the silence she heard Adam say, "I'm going to see Mr. Stint. I want my car back."

Her father reached in a pocket. He said, "You best take this, boy."

Adam took the gun in his hand. He hefted it, felt the way it sat in his palm, for it was a small pistol. He felt a strange calmness overtake him. "Could I use your truck one more time?"

The old man opened his mouth to reply but his answer was drowned out by a shout from the porch.

"No!" came the panicked cry, followed by the clatter of peas on the porch floor as Flo leaped to her feet. Her hands clawed convulsively at her bodice, and she fell heavily across the rail. Adam and her father looked up, and both of them were reminded of a rag doll.

Adam had leaped from the stump and was rushing to Flo's side, when he was nearly jerked off his feet by the vise-like grip of the old man's hand on his sleeve, strong still, though it was gnarled and wizened. He was staring at the empty trailer, which he seemed to have noticed for the first time, his old rheumy eyes like bloodshot marbles, "Where's the mower?" he croaked. He glanced over to where Flo lay slumped over the porch railing. "Hun, where's my mower?" "My mower," he was shouting now, "What did you do with my mower?"

¶

Dear Rory,

Tremendous poems. Your best yet, especially the one beginning "Moon rise / The transom of the mind falls open." Do you have periods when you can't leave the house? I sense something of that sort in the poem. It struck a chord with me, as I have been feeling more and more that way myself, wanting to stay home, just say to hell with the whole brouhaha, and then I think thank god for curtains.

All the best,
Andy

¶

Dear Jolie,

I enclose a money order. This is all I'll be sending for a long time. I am preparing to consolidate my mind and enter a forest to live on acorns, thereby turning what's left of my life into a manageable asset. I have had to walk upon the spines of hideous obstacles in order to get this money to you. I have endured gruesome adventures. Essentially, I was flung down and castigated. Morally, I failed, and was embarrassed. Happily, I have slewed forth and triumphed. Details follow.

For the past two months, ever since the bank started snatching its usurer's cut from everything I deposit on the pretense of minutely shrinking the vast unpayable sums I owe it, I have cajoled, threatened, and wheedled the tenants into paying a portion of the rent in cash. On Wednesday last I had five hundred and eighty dollars precisely folded in the outside pocket of my blue jacket (the more secure inside pocket being ripped and dangling). I was walking down Fourth Street on the north sidewalk, on my way to the post office, whistling and swinging my arms, and taking little jumps over the broken spots in the pavement, of which there were a great many. My eyes were darting this way and that, there not being any salient sights on the street to keep them in one place for long, when they fell upon a vehicle idling at a traffic light, smoke eructing from its tailpipe in a stinking cloud. Though I was approaching from behind, and so did not have a full and capacious view of the object in its entirety, various tokens and signs let me know that this was the very vehicle I had seen described in a story by one of my contributors. The engine of my brain gave a small whirr and told me that the knobby thing visible through the grime of the vehicle's rear window was in all likelihood the hatless head of that same contributor. This is called reasoning from the whole to the part; it takes but a second. Having not expected to see said contributor in that spot, and he of course not expecting me there either, I took advantage of these combined unexpectancies to crouch very low and creep up behind the truck (for the vehicle in question was indeed a pickup truck) before the light could flash its permissive green again. My intention was to spring into the bed of the truck—like a tiger, one could say—and then advance rapidly across it to the back of the cab. Once there I had planned—the brain, reinforced by a rapidly pounding heart, was now whirring at a tremendous speed—to clutch with my right hand the chromium mount of a large radio antennae which I saw protruding from the roof while my left arm snaked swiftly around the edge of the cab and slithered in through the open window at the driver's side. It would have been a good surprise had it worked. Unfortunately, at the very instant I launched myself into the air in the direction of the bed of the truck it disappeared beneath me. The light had leaped abruptly to green (there is, alas, no yellow in that direction), and the truck had shot forward with a great squealing and smoking of its tires. I might have lost my balance at that moment. That I did not, at least not yet, and was able to bound in hot pursuit, was due to nothing but sheer luck. I believe I was waving my arms and yelling, and was even gaining on the truck, which had been held up by traffic, when I was betrayed by the sole of my shoe. I should have mentioned this at the outset: part of my left shoe had been relaxing its grip on the other parts for several days now and was making a regular flapping sound when I walked. It was a rather enjoyable noise and I had learned to smack my foot down in a way that amplified it several fold. It was quite a stunner in the supermarket. Of course I had not considered the dangers this would pose should I ever need to accelerate my pace beyond a hobble, as indeed I did need to do when pursuing the truck. Thanks to it, the situation did not unfold the way I had hoped when I began to pump the old pistons. To make a long tale short, I fell—precipitously, abysmally, and very hard. I ripped both knees of my trousers, I scraped my left palm so badly it burned like fire for several hours while oozing droplets of blood from parallel furrows, and I almost broke my finger.

So there I was sprawled in the middle of the busy intersection, traffic was backing up in all directions. Amazingly, no one leaped to my aid, nor did they saunter to it. What they thought of course I could not know; perhaps they thought of both leaping and sauntering, but in the end could not be bothered. I could see heads poking out of car windows all down the line, craning for a better view, and not just children's heads either, but still nobody got out. I managed to haul myself up into a sitting position and was engaged in close communication with my knees, when a car horn sounded from far down the line, a single halfhearted toot made by the pressure of an uncertain and craven palm. I looked up. I may have glowered. I am sure I grimaced (I was beginning to register the pain in my hands and knees). I realized that I had lost a shoe, the villain with the flap. I tried unsuccessfully to put it on. I would have had to loosen the lace, which I always double knot. I scarcely had the use of my fingers, paralyzed as they were by tingles. Meanwhile, there was no further sounding of horns. I would have preferred a chorus of them. The drizzle of patient silence was completely unnerving. Swiveling my head to all points of the compass, I saw no manly hand outstretched to help, no angelic smile of succoring female beamed its sunshine upon me. My gaze met only the grinning chrome of the automobiles' grills and bumpers and the blank stares of their huge glass eyes. I crawled—yes, crawled!—on all fours, on my bloodied knees and hands, out of the roadway. I collapsed in a heap on the grass verge. I leaned my back against a signal pole and watched the traffic resume its wonted pace. I thought of how the indifference at the heart of the machine migrates into the souls of those who command them. Then I took off my other shoe and walked home in my socks.

I assumed at first that my finger was only sprained. But after lying awake all night listening to its complaints, I discovered in the morning an interesting new object protruding from my palm: a soft whitish cylinder about twice the thickness of my erstwhile digit. Where I had once had a knuckle, it sported a dimple. I thought, "I ought to have this looked at." Other days I would have carried it to Dorfmann. I would have relished handing him my poor damaged digit like baby Jesus cradled in a bloody palm. There was a time when this would have moved him. But our relationship has hit a sharp snag since you left—he was always soft on you—and I am not going to trust an asshole with the life of my trigger finger. Looking in the phone book I discovered a Lawrence Swindell, MD with an office on Oak Court, which is the little street that runs along the back of the Maytag plant. I swallowed six aspirin and drove over. Oak Court is a dead-end street with small ranch houses along one side and a chain-link fence along the other. A wooden sign—Dr. Lawrence Swindell, MD—hung beneath a mailbox in front of one of the houses.

I opened the screen door, and a chime sounded from somewhere in the back. The waiting room looked like somebody's living room, complete with sofa and glass-topped coffee table. I sat down in a chair by the door. There were not any magazines, and I was the only customer, so I thought I would take a fresh look at my knees. Unfortunately, I had changed pants and the ones I was wearing did not have openings in the right places. I had to roll the legs up almost to my thighs in order to get a really good peek, and because of my hurt finger I had to do the rolling with one hand, which took some time. I palpated the crusty bits on my kneecaps a while, and then I studied my finger some more. It looked a lot like an enormous grub worm. I took out my pen and gave it two little eyes. I was considering the kind of mouth it wanted—a downturned one certainly, it being a wounded creature, but I wasn't sure if it should have teeth—when I was interrupted by the entrance of a woman in a nurse suit. I thought of poor Mama and Mrs. Robinson. Seeing me there with my pants rolled up she assumed that I had come about my knees and was already bending over for a closer look when I said, "No, my knees are O.K. It's my trigger finger." I held it up so she could look at it. I rotated it so she could see all sides. "It has eyes," I said.

"I see that," she replied.

I said, "Do you know Elaine Robinson?"

"I don't think so," she said. "Should I?"

I thought she should. I said, "Elaine Robinson is a nurse in Milwaukee."

She said, "Why would I know somebody in *Milwaukee*? I've never even been to *Chicago*."

I wanted to tell her why, but the reason evaded me. "Chicago," I said, "is bigger than Milwaukee." She looked puzzled. So I went on, "It started with my shoe." I lifted my left foot and shook it. The loose sole flapped open and shut. I made it do that a few times. "It's trying to say something," I explained.

She opened her mouth, then closed it. I heard a toilet flushing, and a moment later the doctor walked into the waiting room. He was smiling broadly and ratcheting a bountiful paunch down with successive jerks of a narrow belt. A final cinch, and the belt disappeared into a fold of his belly. He was fat, but except for the paunch there was not a lot of roundness to him. He was blockish and large and his huge square head was bald right down to the ears, which were small and lay flat against his skull. I thought of my own ears and wanted to cuff them (I mean my ears, but also his). "What we got here?" he boomed. I exhibited my offended digit, which he bent over and studied, furrows of fat forming across his brow, while the nurse looked on, her hands on her hips.

"Can you bend it?" he asked. I tried to make the finger curl; it protested, but I compelled it over. While the doctor interrogated my finger, my own gaze was fixed on the top of his glabrous pate hovering just inches from my face. Round and smooth as a bowling ball, about that size, it was so shiny it made me blink. I glanced up and saw the nurse had noticed my fascination. A faint smile touched the corners of her mouth. Then she winked. I noticed for the first time how neatly she fit her uniform.

The doctor straightened. "Might be broken," he said. "But if it is, then the bone's still in place. Otherwise, you couldn't move it like you did. Anyway, I can't put a cast on till the swelling has gone down."

I followed him into the examination room. With my pants still rolled above the knees, I looked as if I were about to wade in something. He had me sit on a polished metal table. My feet dangled several inches off the floor. I felt like a child in a high chair. I kicked my legs back and forth in an attempt to pump the feeling up a little.

"Stop that," he said. Which was of course the perfect thing to say.

I sat quietly while he packaged my finger in a splint constructed of two tongue depressors wrapped with several turns of adhesive tape. Then without a word he grasped the rolled legs of my trousers and turned them back down, first one and then the other, and snapped the cuffs straight with sharp tailor-like jerks. He must have worked in a clothes store before becoming a doctor. Leaning on the table next to me he wrote out a prescription for pain medicine.

The whole time the doctor was applying the splint the nurse had just stood there watching, hands on her hips, and now she said, "That'll be twenty dollars."

I had the wad of bills from yesterday in my pants pocket, where I had transferred it that morning. My intention was to reach down and peel off a twenty without dragging the rest to the surface. This was not as simple as I thought. Because of the splint I was forced to use my left hand, the clumsy one, though the money was in my right pocket. By twisting my shoulders and torso I contrived to work my hand down into the pocket, where I attempted to unfold the wad. I had what I thought was the corner of a single bill pinched between my thumb and index, while my other three fingers fought off a dozen other bills clinging to it. But the more I struggled, the more tangled they became. From the corner of my eye I could see the nurse craning her neck in what was either astonishment or an effort to peer into my pocket. I succeeded finally in peeling off the twenty and began cautiously withdrawing my hand. This hand, however, having approached the pocket from the wrong side, had entered at an oblique angle, and was now stuck there. I could, of course, let go the bill, relax my fingers, and slip my hand out without difficulty. That, however, would defeat the purpose, leave me without the twenty, and oblige me to start the whole process over. One solution would have been for the doctor or, better, the nurse, being smaller, to put her hand in. But I was reluctant to have them do that. Meanwhile, my awkward posture (twisted at the middle, my left hand sunk deep in my right pocket), combined with the physical exertion of trying to wrench the hand back out, caused me to lose my balance. Staggering sideways, I lurched across the room and collided with the side of a glass-fronted cabinet. Fortunately the glass did not break, though judging by the noise a number of things fell over inside. Finally, by dint of an upward jerk that practically lifted my feet from the floor, I snatched my hand free from what I had come to think of as the jaws of my pocket. My hand rocketed forth, the sought-after twenty dangling from it, and immediately in its wake the entire wad of remaining bills erupted from the pocket in a kind of volcanic explosion.

I recall a moment of paralysis. No one moved, and there was no sound other than the leaf-like flutter of money falling to the floor. I shouted "That's *my* money!" And the next moment we were all three knocking heads as we crawled around the floor on our hands and knees. I mashed the doctor's hand under my knee. He hit me in the temple with his bowling ball. The nurse was swinging her hips like battering rams. It was clear that he, with his hanging paunch, and I, with my damaged finger, had no chance against her. We exchanged looks that said as much, and scrambled to our feet. The doctor handed me the tuft of bills he had gathered. We walked over and stood against the wall to be out of her way, and watched while she finished the job. Wagging her hips, she crawled around the floor like a dog on a scent. Spy a bill and she would pounce, slap it with the flat of her hand like a child slapping jacks, hand it across to the steadily growing wad crumpled in her fist, and lunge for another. The doctor shot me a glance that I interpreted as smirking. I winked, and he looked away. I thought of how I would feel if that were you on the floor, and I was embarrassed for him.

Having captured all the bills in sight, she spent a minute or two sniffing in corners and behind the desk. Then she stood up, brushed the dust from her knees, and handed me the crumpled wad of bills. It was warm and damp from her fist, and I hastened to stuff it into my left pocket, making sure it went all the way to the bottom. I remembered my father on the front lawn of our house stuffing a dead mole into his pocket, an event I had forgotten until that instant. I think I must have paused a few moments, hand in pocket, lost in reverie. When I looked up again, I noticed she was still holding one twenty-dollar bill. I know some people— and I suspect you are among them—would say that this was just the twenty dollars I owed her, and I suppose that was the way she saw it. But that's not the way I saw it. I accidentally had spilled some money on the floor, and this woman had helped pick it up, as was only polite. But now she had decided—unilaterally decided, without a word of consultation with its rightful owner—to keep a portion of it for herself, ignoring the blatant fact that I had not paid her anything yet.

So I held out my hand and said, "Could I have my money please."

She replied, "You owe us twenty. This is the twenty" She waved the bill in my face.

I said, "But I didn't give you *that* twenty," and I dug in my pocket, and, after a little work, I contrived this time to draw forth a single bill. "For all you know, I was going to give you *this* twenty," and I waved that one in *her* face.

"What fucking difference does it make?" she snapped.

The doctor murmured, "Lucille." I realized, from the way he said it, that this was his wife.

I said, "It makes all the difference in the world. The fact of the matter is, I had not yet paid you one penny. It is likely that I had every intention of paying you the full amount, but you didn't know that. You couldn't know that unless you had eyes inside my head. Furthermore, had I chosen not to pay you, you would not have had the right just to snatch it. You would have had to take me to court."

Neither of them had an answer to this. They looked at me, wide-eyed, and then at each other, obviously bewildered by my glibness. I continued in a more conciliatory tone, "Just give it to me, and I'll give it back to you." She hesitated a moment. She looked at the doctor, who shrugged. She was starting to hand it over, when I said coyly, "Maybe."

She jerked her hand back, hiding it behind her like a naughty child with illicit candy. It was an incredibly guilt-admitting gesture. She must have seen it that way too, for she brought her hand back to her side. She looked sullen; she stared at her shoes and would not meet my eyes. I felt a tremendous surge of energy. I held out my hand and spoke in a firm tone.

"Lucille, give me the money. Give it to me now."

Slowly she lifted her hand, still not looking at me. I took the money and said. "Thank you." I let a moment pass, allowing as it were the proof of ownership to settle. Then I said, "Here's the money I owe you," and I handed the other bill to her.

I turned and walked out. I could feel their eyes on me, the darts of their hatred banging the back of my head like steel balls. The waiting room was crowded with people.

On the way home I was elated. Despite the continuing pain in my finger I couldn't resist tapping out little tunes on the car horn.

The finger is not broken, I think. The swelling is almost down, though there seems to be a slight bow below the knuckle that was not there before. I am feeling very light-headed, but I can't sleep. I lie on the sofa downstairs. There is a calmness to the blue light there. Or I sit in the red chair among the boxes. I get the feeling that I am waiting in a station surrounded by my luggage. I am very excited. I ask myself, Where the hell is the train?

Love,

Andy

¶

Dahlberg!

Red Ford Pickup? Alberta license plate? Did you imagine for one instant that I didn't know that was you? You are pushing me too far. I have training in firearms.

Whittaker

OCTOBER

Dear Vikki,

Ever since the school year started a few weeks ago, crowds of children have been walking past my house every morning and afternoon. I don't remember this happening other years, though it must have unless they've changed their route, and why would they do that except to annoy me? No matter where I am inside the house, even in the basement, I can hear them whooping. They evidently enjoy making as much noise as humanly possible. I tell myself I am not the target of this shouting, but am not convinced. Peering out, I catch them shooting glances at my house. Their voices are angular and piercing.

This afternoon, instead of slowly piping on up the street, they stayed across from the house, a stationary vortex of shouts and screams. When this continued undiminished, when, as it seemed to me, it *refused* to stop, I felt my neck and scalp growing warm. I would have spluttered with rage, as they say, had there been anyone around to splutter at. Lifting a corner of my curtain—I had to jerk out a nail to do this—I crouched by the sill and peeked out. Across the street a group of five or six small boys were playing "king of the mountain" on the wide stump of an elm the city sawed down early in the summer. They were taking turns shoving each other off. They kept at it for several minutes, shouting all the while, and then, as if obeying some secret signal, they seemed to grow bored, instantly and all together; they stopped playing, and for a couple of minutes just stood around, talking softly and fidgeting. Now and then one of them would kick the stump. They seemed bewildered. They reminded me of ants when you have moved the honey jar. I was about to rush out—I could already picture myself waving my arms as I charged down the front steps, practically falling down them in my haste, my bare knees (I was in my undershorts) moving up and down like pistons, the children scattering like moths. I had reached the door, when I stopped: they had climbed up on the stump and were standing bunched together there. One boy counted, "one, two, three," and they all let fly in chorus. They did this just once, a single outburst. I don't think it was an actual word; it sounded like "yee-oo." Considering their number it ought to have been deafening, but it was not loud at all. I am not sure how to describe this yell, the half-hearted effort behind it, the visible reluctance of the shouters, the lackluster quality of the sound, except to say that it filled me with discouragement. From my doorway I watched them stagger on up the street in a gaggle, shoving and laughing.

After they had gone, and no other children came, I put on my overcoat and went across the street and stood on the stump. Standing there, I looked back at my house. With the elm no longer shading it, the sun's glare has become intolerable, and I have nailed blue plastic tarpaulins over the windows to shut it out. I looked at the house next door; the curtains were drawn there too, dark red "drapes" in the living room, a yellow fabric with stripes and ruffles in the kitchen. They probably had been pulled shut the night before to prevent persons outside from looking in. When I thought of those neighbors, people I would not recognize if I crossed them in the street, drawing the curtains at night, the woman taking one curtain in each delicate hand and drawing them to her, perhaps after lighting a wood fire in the grate, the words "cozy" and "private" floated into my mind. The blank blue sheets of plastic pulled taut across the windows of my own house, however, when I turned to look at it, occasioned a rather different feeling. I stood a long while trying to put the feeling into words. A single phrase kept popping into my mind: a blind house.

The machine whirs in a semblance of labor, furious and completely useless, since it is not hooked up to anything. I accomplish nothing all day—in effect, I *do* nothing all day—and by evening I am exhausted.

I have sunk back into all my old vices—slovenliness, sloth, and gargantuan pettiness. Smoking three packs a day and I constantly run out. I wander around the house cursing and slapping the empty packs, or I fish butts out of the ashtray. I went to the Arts Council picnic, where I had a fit. And I am writing letters to the *Current* again, despite what happened last time I did that. I enclose my latest. Better not show Chumley—I promised him I wouldn't.

Did I tell you about Sokal's boots? The famous snakeskin ones he was carrying on about? I found them under the stairs in our basement. When I first laid eyes on them I thought they were stuffed carp. It was you, I think, who reported way back then that he was going around telling everyone we had stolen his boots.

Speaking of which, someone has stolen my mailbox. It was a nice wooden box, made to look like a little red barn. They just came up on the porch and unscrewed it. I am sure you remember it: the mail went in through a slot in the roof, and you opened the barn doors to get it out.

We have reached the equinox. I close my eyes and imagine the planet sliding through blackest space, the circle of life spiraling down, no steering wheel, and no brakes. And I don't have any money to heat this house. Not just blind, but cold. Could you spare something?

Love,
Andy

¶

To the Editor:

Just last month I wrote a letter protesting the *Current*'s shameful neglect of our city's most esteemed literary figure, the author and editor Andrew Whittaker. You have now rectified that error, only to tumble into another just as grave. I refer to your coverage of the sensational events at last Saturday's Arts Furtherance League Picnic in Armistice Park ("Arts Picnic Erupts Unexpectedly"). The evident bias in your reporter's choice of adjectives leaves no room for doubt as to whose side *she* is on. For example, in recounting the buildup to the crucial events indexed in the headline, she describes Whittaker's interpellation of a particularly tedious speaker as "butting in." His statements are said to be "outbursts." He does not smile, he "leers." He does not speak, he "shouts incoherently" or "chatters." According to your article, when Whittaker was warned by a policeman to put the platter down, "he [Whittaker] responded with a shrill cackle." I was there, and I dare say considerably closer to Mr. Whittaker than your reporter (who as I recall had taken refuge behind a cedar tree), and I would describe the sound emitted by Whittaker as a guffaw. But of course I was not blinded—or in this case, deafened—by parochial prejudice. I fear we hear what we listen for.

Nor do I agree with the statement that Mr. Whittaker was led away in tears. The beady bits aglitter upon his cheeks were, I believe, droplets of the Chablis that one of the women—a burly one in red shorts—had thrown in his face. When they were forcing him into the car I noticed the crushed paper cup was still lodged in the collar of his jacket. A fitting motif, I must say, for the whole affair. The hurler, it turns out, was a friend of Eunice Baker's, who had read from her new book of poetry earlier in the afternoon. Miss Baker, for the legions who have never heard of her, is co-editor of *The Art News*. It was during her reading that Whittaker climbed onto the stage the first time. According to your reporter, "Whittaker snatched the microphone and began to rail against [Baker's] work." This is scarcely the kind of precision one expects from a professional journalist. As a scientific man, I place a high value on precision. What does it mean to rail? What precisely was said during this particular instance of "railing"? A factual account would run something like this: "Mr. Whittaker, in a loud voice (they had turned off his microphone), but quite calmly, gave a brief critique of Miss Baker's performance in which he described her delivery as 'menopausal mooing' and her poems as 'cow farts.'" Your reporter then says that the audience "reacted with sustained boos." While that is broadly correct, there were at least a couple of young men standing at the back of the crowd who were laughing loudly. The ripples of hilarity from those hearty striplings floated like oriflammes above the general drone and lent a rather different tone to the episode. And this is precisely the point I made in my previous letter: our city and state need people like Whittaker, people who decline to pull their punches and are not afraid to outrage "public opinion" when they believe that opinion to be mistaken. And the people laughing, don't they deserve a champion too?

Whittaker has become the focus of enormous public curiosity in recent years. I know for a fact that he has not sought this out. He is anything but the "publicity hound" caricatured in *The Art News*. In fact he does not read newspapers, nor does he sit around coffee shop tables gossiping.

His fondest wish is to be allowed to labor in peace.

I remain sincerely,

Warden Hawktiter, MD

¶

Dear Mailman,

As you can see, the mailbox is missing. I believe someone stole it. I will be getting another one soon. In the meantime, please slide the mail under the front door. If you look toward the hinge side, you will see the "slot" I cut in the rubber strip that runs along the bottom. If you come across my barn please let me know.

Thanks,

A. Whittaker

¶

Dear Stewart,

I would have preferred meeting with you in your office, where I could put my feet up on your desk, so to speak, and talk man to man, but I don't feel presentable these days. I don't think I could face your receptionist. Nothing serious, no disfiguring disease or rank odor so far as I can tell, though they say the real stinkers have no idea. True, I am not happy with my clothes, especially my shoes, and would like some new ones (money is very tight at the moment). But it's not that either; it's more the feeling I have that whatever is going on inside me has become visible on the surface, in my face, but not just in my face, in my gait. I find I am walking with a stoop most of the time; I seem unable to correct it. Every attempt results in a ridiculous bend in the opposite direction, over backwards, as if I were looking up at an airplane, so I don't even try anymore. I picture myself standing in front of your pretty receptionist, stooped over like that, or the other way, staring up at the light fixture, and in these clothes. I am not sure I would be able to refrain from holding out my hand and asking her for a dollar. I fear this would reflect badly on you, since she knows we are friends, so I am not coming.

I assume you saw the review in the *Current* of my performance at the Arts Furtherance League thingamajig in the park. In case you did not, I enclose the clipping, which you should take with a dollop of salt. The picnic was a lot of fun—I was not "in a rage" as they claim. In fact, I was floating calmly somewhere at the level of the treetops while most of it was happening. The best description of my state would be "blimp-like." I had a marvelous feeling of detached observation even as things were, as the paper said, "in an uproar." I have been charged with disorderly conduct. At first they were going to charge me with assault with a deadly weapon, but I convinced them that while it was true that I was throwing the cold cuts, I had a tight grip on the platter. After the initial scuffle and a rather standoffish ride to the station house—the policeman in front did not like it that I was kicking the back of his seat—they became quite affable. I told them faggot jokes and they bought me a ginger ale. Then they let me go. I have to appear in court at some point, I forget when, and will you go with me? I am embarrassed to ask, since I never apologized for the accident with the vase at Ginny's party. I would apologize now, except that it would look then as if I were doing it only in order to get your legal services for free, which of course they have to be, since I am in a tight spot financially, as I have said already. This seems to be an insoluble social conundrum. It is amazing how, wherever I turn these days, new difficulties spring up. Perhaps we can talk about this after the hearing.

Sincerely,

Andy

¶

Dear Mr. Mailer,

You probably don't know who I am, and that is good, since it allows me to introduce myself without having to fight through a thicket of misconception and prejudice, as is the case here, where I am so well known I am practically invisible. I am the editor of the literary magazine *Soap*, which you have probably never heard of either. I enclose a copy of our most recent issue. We are currently at the beginning of a multiyear project of restructuring and expansion that we expect will establish us as the dominant literary voice in this part of the world, if not nationally. In conjunction with that expansion we are hosting next May or June the First Annual Soap Festival of Literature and the Arts. I won't give a full description of the event here, only say that it will last a full seven days and feature many adjuncts. It will be preceded by colorful brochures. Look for one in your mailbox soon. Of course you probably are thinking, what is in this for me? It is only natural that you should think this, and even ask it boldly, were we in the give and take of conversation or should you be the kind of person who talks back to letters, as I am, as well as to the television. I don't think looking out for one's career is anything to be ashamed of even if this means traveling halfway across the country. It is fortunate that we have air travel. I look after my career too, though it is small, which makes looking after it easier in some ways but much harder in others, since it is difficult to get people to pay attention to you if you are not someone they are paying attention to already, which you are; though, of course, there are a lot more of them for you to have to keep an eye on, and in that respect your job is harder. Am I being clear? The point, which I realize I have been too slow in getting to, is that you have won the Soap Lifetime Achievement Award. Physically, this is a framed photograph of Marilyn Monroe in her bubble bath. It is about the size of a breakfast tray. The frame is fitted with removable rubber feet on the bottom so you can rest it on the mantel, if you want, if that is where you decide to keep it, without fear of it sliding off, or you can take them off and hang it on a wall. Spiritually, it is, or will be in future years, once several people like you have received it, a signal honor.

The award will be presented, or bestowed, at the end of an invitation-only banquet at the historic Grand Hotel. I will make a speech and then you will make a speech. All will then adjourn to the ballroom.

You have the choice of taking a room in that hotel for the duration of your stay (we would hope you will come out for at least a couple of days) at our expense or, better, staying as an honored guest in my home. Your wife is of course welcome too, if you have a wife. I personally do not have a wife. I do have a maid, or had until recently, so you do not have to worry that you will be staying in a filthy bachelor pad. The house is quite large and sits on a pleasant tree-lined street. I was intending to move into a smaller place, and to this end I packed everything up in boxes, except for the few items I need for personal use, which is really just one plate, one cup, and so forth, and of course the furniture. But if you are coming, as I truly hope you will, I will revise my plans. Rest assured, all the stuff will be set back out by the time you get here. There is, however, no way I can put back all the really nice vases and paintings and such my ex-wife took when she left, despite having nowhere to put them, insufficient walls and mantels and such. She has to keep them in storage, which is just an additional unnecessary expense. She does not live that far from you, and if you wanted to find out more about me, you could go and see her. I of course will also answer any questions, for what that's worth.

Mr. Mailer, I want to be frank with you, as I want you to be frank with me in your response, if there is one, as I hope there will be; that is only common courtesy. Perhaps you have a secretary who will respond, or not, as the case may be. Perhaps only a secretary will read this. Perhaps only a secretary *is* reading this. If that is the case, I am not talking to you, but to someone I know even less than you, since he (she?) has not written any books that I have read, or else why would he (she?) be a secretary, even to a famous author. And there you have it. That's always the problem with letters. On the telephone I could say, Is that you, Norman? Of course, having not the least idea what you sound like, I could still be tricked. It is very difficult to get to the bottom of this.

I have not worked out all the details. There is such a chattering in my mind of dates and times, schedules and program notes, it is like having a head full of talkative mice. Of the festival itself I'll just say that it's going to be big. "How big?" you ask, as well you should. Let me drop this small hint in lieu of an answer: there will be elephants.

I look forward to your visit. I anticipate that we will hit it off. The weather will probably be fine and we can sit out in the yard. When my wife was here, we had flowers. After she bolted, I had no time for that. I ran the mower over them and now there is nothing out there but a little grass; it is austere, but I think you will find it agreeable. As I said, there are trees. I don't interact with the neighbors, so I don't think you will have to worry about hordes of autograph hunters racing over. I was on good terms with a crippled lady across the street, but she seems to have moved away. There is also a woman with a blowtorch, and a wounded writer who wants to straighten me out. I do not expect them to impinge on your visit. Though I am not pugilistic, I am quite large.

Should you not be able to accept this award perhaps you know someone who can.

Sincerely,

Andrew Whittaker

¶

Dear Vikki and Chum-Chum,

Just ignore what those people say. I promise, there's absolutely nothing to worry about. I am convinced I have reached a turning point in my life, despite everything, a moment we will all one day look back on as "the threshold of his fruitful years" or something like that.

Much love to you both,
Andy

¶

To the Editor:

Not long ago you were kind enough to print a letter from me in which I sought to convey to your readers my impressions of the "real" Andrew Whittaker—not the controversial author but the neighbor across the street. I certainly never thought I would feel compelled to write again so soon. But a week or so after I mailed that letter you carried a long reportage by Melissa Salzmann on the annual Arts Furtherance League Picnic. I was distressed to read about Andy's breakdown in front of all those people, and I think it was very wrong of them not to let him speak. While I don't for a minute doubt the honesty of Miss Salzmann's description and am sure some people probably were throwing things, I cannot accept that Andy was among them. I just cannot imagine this gentle vegetarian "snatching up a platter of cold cuts." Furthermore, when it comes to behavior toward the female sex, he is the most courtly of men. It boggles credulity that he would deliberately smear two large chocolate handprints on the front of Eunice Baker's blouse, as your reporter alleges. Nevertheless, it seems the police were called, and poor Andy was led away in tears.

This account simply does not jibe with the Andy I know. *That* Andy is a quiet, dignified, private man. The sort of emotional eruptions your reporter describes—shouting, "giving the finger," throwing food, and weeping—are outside the pale of his character. He is a thoroughly old-fashioned English-type gentleman right down to the accent. I know he makes some people feel uneasy when he talks to them in that accent, as they suspect it is some kind of joke but are not sure enough of this actually to laugh. Yet even if, as they suspect, he is being insufferable on purpose, there is a big difference between that and throwing things.

So reading your article I was faced with a dilemma. Either your reporter was mistaken to the point of mendacity, or Andy has suffered a grievous breakdown. I have been a *Current* subscriber for many years and find it impossible to believe that one of your employees would intentionally tell lies, so I am forced to contemplate the latter explanation. In my previous letter I was reluctant to delve into Andy's private life for fear of losing his trust and affection. But now, with this new scandal, I feel, for his sake, that I must speak out whatever the cost. Otherwise, how will people *ever* understand him?

In that letter I described the many kindnesses he has shown me since an accident left me alone and without the use of both legs. He was married during most of this period, and I could not help observing that it was not a happy marriage, though he never actually spoke of it. He probably thought I had enough troubles of my own without having to listen to his. His wife was a woman of callused sensibilities, vain, avaricious, and strikingly beautiful in a brittle way. Her beauty must have blinded poor Andy. He treated her like a princess. Though never a wealthy man, he owned a thriving business which could have kept them both in modest comfort had she restrained herself a little. But she always had to have more—more clothes, including a leather suit, bigger cars, more lavish vacations, a bigger television. It didn't take her long to "ruin" poor Andy, and then to cast him off like an old shoe. He struggled to keep the business afloat—and his wife in the pink—and this effort devoured the time and energy he needed for his real work. And that is the tragic part. The world will probably never know what it lost in those years.

Though Andy showered me with daily kindnesses—always something, if only a smile—his wife never showed the least consideration for an afflicted neighbor. She would stroll past my house on her way to sunbathe in the park (she was always deeply tanned) and would not even look my way, no matter how loudly I tapped on the windowpane. And I saw things. While I would never spy, she was scarcely private. And she knew I was at the window, even if she refused to acknowledge my taps. It broke my heart to see her comings and goings with men half her age, and then later to see him arrive home, whistling as he walked, lost in a literary cloud perhaps, or studying a leaf he had picked up from the sidewalk. Those were the early days, of course, before he found out. I think I should not say more.

Later, after he knew, after the stormy months, and her eventual departure by motorcycle for greener pastures, I could see the changes in him. No more whistling in the street. Yet he kept doggedly at his work, at his desk at six a.m. every day, even on weekends. I have many solitary hours to while away, and the antics of the little brown birds I sometimes see in the trees and bushes outside my window have helped keep me amused. For this reason I have a pair of powerful binoculars always at the ready. Fearful for Andy ever since his wife left, I would sometimes seize him in the lenses of my instrument as he worked at his desk by an upstairs window. I hoped in this way to catch his downward dips before they had gone too far. A few years ago, I would have seen a man calmly writing, perhaps pausing now and then to stare thoughtfully out the window, the kind of man an earlier age would have dubbed "a literary gent." He might, at most, chew the end of his pencil or scratch a wayward ear. No more! Now what I often see is a face twisted in response to what I can only surmise are unbearable inner torments. His expressions and gestures have become outsized, exaggerated, even grotesque—they reminded me of the histrionic contortions one sees in old silent movies. He will open his mouth and draw his lips back from his teeth in a hideous leer, or he will work his lower jaw back and forth as if testing it for injury. At other times he tears at the little tufts of hair on the sides of his head, just above his ears, as if trying to pull his poor skull apart. He snaps pencils and even ballpoint pens in two, sometimes with his teeth, and throws or spits the pieces out the window. He writes madly for a few minutes and then crosses out what he has written, crosses it out so furiously his upright elbow wiggles in the air as if he were stirring a bowl of thick batter. Sometimes he balls up the page and stuffs it in his mouth. It is horrible.

Meanwhile, the attacks on him have only gotten worse. Because of my affliction, I no longer attend art events. But still I have always made small annual contributions to our Area Arts Furtherance League, even after Andy told me it was a racket. In return for those contributions I received a subscription to *The Art News*, their monthly newsletter. A year or so ago they began a cartoon series called "The World of Winkstacker," which is obviously based on Andrew. He is cruelly pictured with a huge body and a little bullet head, always in shorts that are much too tight for him, and he is made to say the most idiotic things. These are hurtful caricatures, and vulgar as well, with all sorts of sexual overtones, and I don't know how the person who draws them can sleep at night. Next year I am not going to give the Area Arts Furtherance League one penny of my money. I don't understand how those people, many of whom probably go to church, where they worship a god who was persecuted by people just like them, can have so little sympathy for Andy.

I had noticed in the past month or so a new glint in his dull gaze. I knew it was the sign of a man being driven to the edge. To the edge of what I could not tell exactly, though the glint resembled only too closely the one my husband had in his eyes the night he got behind the wheel for the last time. From your article I learned that in Andy's case it was the edge of breakdown! Let those who hate him snicker. The rest of us will grieve.

Sincerely,

Dyna Wreathkit

¶

Dear Fern,

Scarcely two weeks have gone by since I last wrote. In that letter I was still able to talk of the festival with my usual pugnacious gaiety. Nothing has happened since then, and yet everything has happened, and the sentiments I blurted out there seem now as outdated and as indecipherable to myself as yesterday's old newspaper left out in the rain and turning to pulp on the lawn. I have not been frank with you. I have not been frank with myself. The fact is, my life's vehicle seems to have swerved into a cul-de-sac. I have run it against a brick wall. It looks just like the wall behind my elementary school, where they used to make me stand while they threw things at me. I do not wish to stand there any longer.

I have fought for other writers—for Art itself—for over ten years against the puritanical and philistine efforts of the so-called educated class of this state to kill it. Enveloped in the stiffened corduroy of their prejudices, I was practically suffocated, though I struggled against them even as I was strangled. I have been reviled, ridiculed, reduced, and, yes, rendered in crudely drawn cartoons by time-servers, lickspittles, and female baboons. I dug a foxhole—it was called *Soap*—and from it I fired upon the armed phalanges of the Citizens for the Promotion of Pleasantness, the sinister brigades of the Arts Furtherance League, the skirted hordes from the Poets and Painters Mutual Regurgitation and Masturbation Cliques. And all the while, to keep body and soul together while I did this work for which I have never received a penny, I have been compelled to go door to door in an effort to collect absurdly low rents from ungrateful and malingering tenants who have no regard for other people's property, who think nothing of responding to doorbells in their torn underwear, and who, when I show any signs of weakness, attack me with incendiary devices and large pieces of concrete. Wherever I turn, the eyes of the police are on me, while deranged authors are allowed to lurk in the bushes behind my house. I have fallen down, and no one has picked me up. I have seen my trigger finger permanently mangled by a medical charlatan. I am surrounded by boxes. And now finally I have had enough. I have learned to spell B-A-S-T-A! I shall without shame abandon the field to my enemies, fertile as it is with their gore. I say, Let them chortle. Let them whinny with satisfaction. I have my books to write. I am going to think of my own happiness . . .

I don't know how to go on with this letter, or even if I should go on with it. I wonder, wouldn't it be better to ball it up, as I have several others, and toss it onto the little pyramid in the corner? As each crumpled wad lands on top of the pile, and rolls inevitably to the bottom, I think what a metaphor for my life that is, landing on top and rolling helplessly to the bottom. What Author, I wonder, has tossed me here? I look up, as have many before me, hoping to find an answer Up There, but discover only a cracked plaster ceiling and a lampshade of frosted glass enveloped in cobwebs. I live, as perhaps I've told you, alone in an old Victorian house. There is an ornate and stately gloominess about it. And tonight it is so very quiet. The proverbial pin, should it drop, would fall like thunder here. I can hear my own breathing. Stertorous, labored with emotion: were it not my own it would frighten me. Apart from this, the only sounds are the ticking of the grandfather clock—which always reminds me of Mama, since it was her clock—and the dull thud of my slippers as I pad to the bathroom or trudge numbly into the kitchen in pursuit of another drink. Another drink to give me courage! I sit and think. I write with a ballpoint, so there is no ancient scratching of the quill or even fountain pen, and no ticking of snowflakes at the windowpanes either, as there would have been were I Chekhov and this Russia, though now and then there is the dry rustle of paper. That at least has not changed. I raise the glass to my lips, and I am startled by the bitter cachinnation of the ice cubes. How can I, whose business is words, be suddenly at a loss for them? I chew my pen tip. I gnaw and I dream. I have strange fantasies. I see you sitting in a rocker, in a blue flower-print nightgown, your feet in slippers, perhaps those comical little slippers made to look like bunnies with plastic eyes and pink ears, while I read to you from my translation of Catullus. Does that seem far-fetched to you? You say nothing about the discrete words of affection I inserted in two previous letters. I am bewildered. Were they too subtle, and you overlooked them? Were they too strong, and you cringed? Were they too clumsy, and you tripped over them? In my anguish I gnaw furiously and spit bits of plastic onto the floor.

When you say Crawford posed you, do you mean with his *hands*? I see him, out-of-shape, flabby, and drooling. I see his pot belly, that vile pumpkin, bulging his shirt buttons. Do not defend him! I see his filthy bloodshot eye peeping through the view-finder. What do you mean by "in on the ground floor"? On the floor of his house? Does he even have a house, or was it on the filthy carpet of his trailer? The images pour in like water through a ruptured dike. I hold my head in my hands and want to roll on the floor. Listen to me, Fern! I know all about cameras. I once owned a Leica M3.

Andy

¶

My dear Fern,

So much has been happening lately, both good and bad, and I feel up to my ears in it. I started a letter to you yester-day. No, I finished a letter to you last night. I even dropped it through the slot in the mailbox, only to plunge my arm after it. I retrieved the letter but managed to put a nasty scrape on the back of my hand. I have not been able to work up the reading list you asked for, though yesterday I made a start on that as well. I haven't heard anything from you about my invitation. I need to hear something soon. Your silence seems part of a larger breakdown of organization. I haven't slept, and now it's morning. I am not at all tired. I know it sounds preposterous, but I am not able to shake the conviction that I won't need to sleep again. I am sitting at the kitchen table with a fresh cup of coffee. Out the window I can see sunlight on the tops of the taller trees. I have been looking at the pictures in an illustrated encyclopedia of mammals that I keep on the kitchen table in order to have something to stare at while I eat. I sat down with the intention of telling you about the death of my mother, about my mother who recently died, as I think I must have mentioned, and how I feel about her and it, and also probably something about my sister and father, as they were part of the picture, since I don't have anyone handy to talk to, but I have changed my mind, and I am going to tell you about the tree sloth instead, since this is a creature I feel personally very close to.

Tree sloths are misunderstood by almost everyone, including the so-called scientific community, where people are supposed to try and understand just such hard-to-understand facts as these unprepossessing creatures, who, unlike kangaroos, don't wear their souls on their sleeves. Nature's penchant for malicious impishness, which is evident in so many places, is an aspect that constantly eludes the scientific mind, plodding humorlessly on as it does, and the failure to grasp this penchant has made a deep understanding of the sloth impossible, since they are, in my view, the tragic victims of one of nature's cruelest jokes.

Far from being the sulking solitaries portrayed in animal picture books, sloths are at heart amazingly outgoing fellows (I almost wrote "little fellows," though of course they are quite large; it is just that one grows to really like them and "little fellows" seems to capture that feeling). In fact, they are by nature more gregarious than dogs. Yet who has ever heard of a pack of sloths? And while brimming with a desire to wag, they have no tail with which to do it, an absence that is pretty much a compendium of their difficulties. Instead of gamboling in bunches they are condemned (this is the trick part) to pass all their days in complete solitude, spending the handful of waking hours nature grants them each day creeping with glacial slowness among the branches of a single great tree, to the point that some observers go nearly crazy with boredom just watching them. Of that one tree consist their house, their city, their world.

Of course they hate this. For not only are they sociable to a fault, they are also quick-witted—in more favorable circumstances one would say they were bright as buttons—and the larval slowness at which they are condemned to crawl, and the tedium of the scenery they pass at a snail's pace, not to mention the simple injustice of it all, drives them wild. In fact they often go insane, the only species besides man in which insanity occurs on a regular basis. Indeed, among sloths insanity is so widespread we should probably regard it as their normal state, with mental balance—found in any case only during their first year or two of existence, before a full awareness of their condition breaks in upon them—a youthful aberration.

As they hitch along a branch they nibble now and then from the thick foliage that surrounds them in suffocating green clouds, thoroughly masticating one leaf before inching on to the next. One can imagine how tasteless such a monotonous diet must seem after a few years, and how sick of it they become. In fact starvation is believed to be the leading cause of death among adult sloths, when they just can't get any more of it down. As a natural expression of all this, indeed as its inevitable consequence, the sloth has acquired what is without doubt the most pitiable cry in the whole animal kingdom. As they wend their way among the leaves they emit a constant series of small desperate squeaks from their noses. They do this by stopping their nostrils with two of their large flat toes. They then attempt to exhale vehemently through the nose until they build up considerable internal pressure, which they release with explosive effect by suddenly jerking both toes free of the nostrils with a swift forward motion. The resulting wiffle, though not exactly loud, has extraordinary carrying power. And it conveys such an extreme of pathos and grief that the native people will cover their ears and flee rather than listen to it for a second, even if this means abandoning the bananas or whatever it is they are carrying, perhaps a warthog they had just speared and had hoped to bring home to feed a numerous family. They would much prefer the wailing of a hut full of hungry children, though it last for many hours, to even one instant of the cry of the sloth! The sloth, for its part, appears not to have any ears and so probably can't hear itself, the only silver lining in the creature's cloudy existence. Unable ever to find anything new or remotely interesting in its tree, which though huge is still just one tree, the sloth finally gives up trying altogether, losing even the will to stuff a pair of fat toes up its nostrils. At which point it enters its final stage, known as "the great silence," when it hangs all day upside down. Wrapped in silent gloom it sinks deeper and deeper into an imaginary world of fond companions and giddy social life. Colonies of insects breed in its fur and it does not move a paw to scratch. Gradually a thick green moss grows over it, until it is scarcely more than a green bump on a branch, until one day, absorbed in its dreams, it forgets to hold on and plunges to its death on the forest floor.

I have learned to imitate the sloth's cry almost exactly. I am able to do this, I think, because I have been upside down for so long. When I am not upside down I am bathing.

Andy

¶

Dear Vikki,

Sorry to have taken this long to answer your letter, which was so kind, so full of real concern, and to thank you for the money. I was laid up for four days last week with what I guess was food poisoning. I had found a pack of franks at the back of the fridge, where they had been for God knows how long, as I had stopped opening the refrigerator quite some time ago, not expecting anything to be in there. I thought they would be safe to eat if I cut the blue parts off, but apparently not. I dragged a quilt and pillow into the bathroom and slept on the floor there. Regular geysers at both ends, and horrible cramps. I really thought I was dying. I thought of trying to get to the hospital but that seemed too much bother, as I would have had either to drive myself or crawl to a neighbor's. I am glad now that I don't have a telephone, because I'm sure I would never have had the fortitude not to call you had this been possible. I hate thinking how I might have had you and Chumley racing down here, knowing what it would have cost you both. Lying there on the linoleum I was bothered less by the prospect of dying than by the thought that, if I died, I had wasted my life.

Then, almost suddenly, it was over. At four a.m. I was gasping my last, and at seven I was well, not fit as a fiddle but fit to walk downstairs while clinging tightly to the banister. Morning light was pouring in at the kitchen window. I toasted a piece of stale bread. I have never tasted anything so delicious. I think I'll take a few days off.

Much love to you both,
Andy

¶

To the Editor:

I was disappointed by the *Current's* coverage of this year's Arts in the Park picnic. The errors were manifold and grievous. They piled one upon another, rolling down the slopes of verisimilitude, picking up platitudes and bits of gossip along the way, to land at our feet in the shape of a large comic ball. By "our feet" I mean mine and my husband Henry's. The cascade of misprisions began with Melissa Salzmann's article purporting to describe the events, and was amplified by the familiar irate bombast of Dr. Hawktiter and the vague musings of one Dyna Wreathkit. The resulting large mendacious ball, as I mentioned, finally rolled to a stop at our feet. When Henry and I opened it you can imagine our surprise at finding poor Andrew Whittaker curled up inside, in the sadly reduced state of tabloid fodder. As two people who were present at the picnic, *témoins occulaires*, if you will allow some French, without personal axes to grind, your article and the subsequent letters left us wondering if we were ocular observers at the same occasion.

In recent years, ever since returning from Henry's last post in Zurich, we have spent most of our time at the ranch, where he can concentrate on his inventions without worrying about the neighbors. But still we make a point of coming into town for the arts picnic every year. And every year I am beset by a hope that the large sums that Henry, as a native Rapid Fallsian, feels he must lavish on the several arts organizations that flood our mailbox with ritual pleas will show some signs of bearing fruit. And if not fruit, then flowers or a few meager buds. But there is never anything, and after wandering hopelessly among the craft stalls and standing glumly in front of paintings and sculptures in the big tent while Henry was being fawned over, I saw that this year was going to conform to type. I was very disappointed. Henry sends these people *a lot* of money. There was, however, as we discovered shortly after setting up our little picnic on the grass, one lively innovation in the offing, though it owed nothing to any of the groups that are always after him. The poetry readings had just begun and I was easing Henry down on our quilt, taking care not to let him sit on the ice bucket, when our attention was arrested by the figure of a large unkempt man with an oddly small head emerging rapidly, loping really, from the woods at the edge of the park. It was, we learned later, the writer and publisher Andrew Whittaker. At first we took him for a vagrant or hobo, from the look of his clothes—his trousers had big ragged holes in both knees—and from the way he dug into the items at the food table, as if he had not had a square meal in weeks. Though it sounds cruel to admit, it was entertaining just to watch him go at it. We seldom see out-of-the-ordinary things at the ranch, and Henry was delighted. The man at first seemed totally absorbed in the potato salad, forking it up with his fingers. Then he spent considerable time stuffing his jacket pockets full of brownies, or should I say "trying to," for he seemed to want to get more of them in than his pockets could hold, and whenever one fell out on the ground, as happened repeatedly, he would stamp on it and grind it into the grass with the toe of his shoe. For a long while after that he just stood there munching. He seemed to be in a kind of trance, or dozing on his feet. And then, suddenly, for no reason that we could see, he came alive again. He snatched up a folding chair, and carrying it high above his head, made his way through the crowd of picnickers sitting on blankets around the performance stage, high-stepping over people's heads and walking on their blankets. He was wearing snakeskin boots in which he seemed to be having trouble walking. He was saying "excuse me, excuse me" in a loud voice, and tottering side to side in a way that caused some of the people in his path to scramble off on all fours, and all the while the poet up on the stage was trying to say her poem. She had to speak louder so people could still hear her, but his excuse-mes just got louder too, for he had a booming voice, though she had a microphone. She was shouting by the time he reached the foot of the stage, where he unfolded the chair with a bang (it was a metal chair) and sat down. He slouched down really, his arms flung across his chest and his legs sprawled out in front of him. This was a very provocative posture, and we could tell that things were about to take an interesting turn.

But interesting is too weak a word for what happened next. The events themselves were described accurately enough in your sanctimonious article and later in the earnest and typically obtuse letter from Dr. Hawktiter. The two agree more or less on the bare facts. But bare facts must be clothed by context, and indeed without context are nothing, as everyone knows if they think about it for one second. In the end both so-called eyewitnesses miss the point by miles, and they miss it for the same reason: they take for granted that Whittaker had somehow "lost it" or, in the words of the policeman quoted in your article, that he had "blown a fuse." The only difference between them is whether, generally speaking, they approve of him or not, whether they are, in other words, "on his side" or not. Neither seems to suspect that maybe he had not "lost it" at all, that he was in perfect control, not just of himself but of the audience as well, that all his fuses were intact, and that the whole episode might just be his own far-out contribution to the art exhibit. I believe, *au contraire*, that Whittaker, through the orchestrated chaos of his multiple interventions, amid a dreary chorus of boos only faintly elevated by the laughter of two young men at the back of the crowd, and Henry's giggles, was attempting to force the assembled picnickers to ask themselves the question everybody in America seems to be asking himself and herself today, namely, What is art? Is it a picture frame encrusted with quaint and colorful seashells or small pine cones painted silver? Is it a poem about a dying grandmother's slippers, however sad and worn and yet still pink in places? Is it a painting of buffalos up to their knee-joints in a sea of vanished sawgrass or whatever that stuff is? Or is it cold cuts sailing like Frisbees above all that? I leave this question for your readers to ponder. In the meantime Henry has already pondered it and will know where to send *his* money next year.

Sincerely,

Kitten Hardway

¶

Dear Harold,

I have definitely decided to pay you a visit as soon as I can find the right outfit.

Meanwhile I am going to tell you another funny story. Across the street from my house stands an ugly brick duplex, a featureless box with a metal awning above the front door. The ground floor is occupied by a woman alone— faded, middle-aged, and in a wheelchair. Her skin is so pale it looks bleached. Though her apartment must have several rooms, she spends all her time in a single room fronting the street. The television is always turned on in that room, yet I have never observed her watching it. I have never seen her reading. She looks out the window instead, hour after hour. Even at night I have noticed her with her forehead pressed against the glass. She sometimes looks bare-eyed, as it were, but just as often she is peering through the largest binoculars I have ever seen. She looks quite frail, emaciated even. The binoculars must be extremely heavy, and it is a wonder she can hoist them to eye level, much less hold them there without shaking. That she is able in fact to do this for long minutes at a time I can personally attest, since I have spent many odd moments over the years enclosed in their inquisitive circles. At almost any hour of the day, if I peer across at her house, she will be at the window, swiveling her glasses in my direction the instant she catches sight of me. With her pointed chin, blunt nose, and triangular face widening upward to the huge bulging lenses where her eyes should be, and with the skinny rachitic arms supporting the binoculars jutting outward at each side of her head, she reminds me of an enormous fly, an enormously quizzical fly. I would not be surprised to hear her buzzing. Yet in her comportment she is more like a spider. Take even the most banal occurrence on our very ordinary street—a postman walks past, whistling perhaps, or cursing softly, as usual; or a bushy-tailed squirrel scampers up an oak tree or digs for an elusive morsel in the grassy margin between the sidewalk and the street; or even, given the prodigious magnification of her instrument, a small insect, perhaps a ladybug with attractive spots, laboriously climbs a utility pole—and she pounces instantly upon it, twirling the focus knob until she has it clinched in the death grip of her hemispheres. Her curiosity seems never to slacken, and, depending on one's mood and how one feels about being watched from close up, a stroll down our street can be comforting or terrifying. The tedium of a life driven to such behavior is painful to contemplate. I, of course, cannot help but contemplate it every time I look in that direction, which I can hardly refrain from doing and still find my way off the block. So far as I can tell, she never goes out of her apartment, and almost never out of that one street-fronting room, and no one except delivery people and occasionally some sort of nurse ever goes in. I could, of course, pay her little visits, little drop-ins with cookies and a good book, and I have considered it once or twice, but I know I never shall. I am afraid of becoming entangled with someone so needy, caught as it were by those pincerlike arms. I realize that this sounds heartless, and in the end I have come up with something which I think is considerably more entertaining than a visit. I put on little shows for her instead. I call them episodes.

The theater is my own upstairs window. Directly in front of it I have placed a small desk at which I sit and pretend to write (I do my actual writing at the kitchen table). I am quite deliberate about this. I pull out the chair, sit down, take up a pencil, test the point, go to the window and sharpen it, leaning out so the shavings will drift down to the street. I return to my desk, draw up the chair, adjust the angle of the blank sheet in front of me, and I begin to write. I am never more than seconds into this ritual before I feel the focus of her attention on me. Perhaps I should say the *clamp* of her attention on me, since I often experience a small jolt at the precise moment I am snapped into focus, or surmise that I have been snapped into focus, since of course I am not in a position to actually witness that occurrence, if it is an occurrence. In any case, the jolt is so slight, even faint, that I am not sure whether I should call it a mental jolt or a physical jolt. It is possible, of course, that I am merely imagining a jolt or—and this seems most likely of all—that I experience an actual jolt but only as a consequence of having imagined myself suddenly snapping into focus. Be that as it may, what is certain is that following the jolt, or the imagination of a jolt, I feel myself growing large and curiously foreshortened—I seem to be sitting at the window and yet I am pressed against the closet door behind me. I am sure that, however uncomfortable it may be for me, from her side this foreshortening gives a nice stagy appearance to the episodes.

Head bent over my page, I steal a surreptitious glance, through my eyebrows as it were, at the window across the street. And there they are, as always, the dual circles of her lenses aimed right at me. I scribble a few sentences, and I pause. I gnaw at the eraser. My face brightens—I have just discovered the perfect formulation!—and I return to the page with new vigor. I am now writing rapidly. I let my tongue protrude between my teeth as a visible sign of mental effort. I am conscious of her gaze burning on my cheek, tracing the line of my lips, dwelling on my tongue, examining my fingernails. I continue in this vein for some time, a model of the assiduous scribbler, in order to lull my audience, as it were, and leave her defenseless before the onslaught, which I am already rehearsing in my mind, even as I pretend to write calmly.

When I judge the moment ripe, when a second glance across the street catches a slight wavering in the rigidity of her instrument, a nodding off as it were, suggestive of faltering attention, I begin to shake my head from side to side, as if crying No! No! to some hidden injunction. This is the first, and still relatively mild, manifestation of the creative throes which will soon hold me helpless in their awful grip. I thrash as if assaulted by insects. I make the most hideous grimaces you can imagine. I tear at my hair, roll my eyes, bite my lips, and howl. One moment I am trying to twist my ear off, and the next I am pounding my head against the table and sobbing. I once let myself go too far during the pounding, and next morning discovered a purple bulb on my forehead that persisted for several days. One day I bit my pencil in half and spit the pieces out the window. This proved so effective—I could see her bouncing in her chair with excitement—that I repeated it in subsequent episodes. It provided a nice dramatic finale to my performances. But of course it could not continue to have the same effect day after day. Like any addict, my audience would require ever-increasing doses in order to experience the same kicks, and maintaining that high level of performance has demanded all my ingenuity. Sometimes, unable to sleep, I get up in the night and rehearse in the bathroom in front of the mirror. I have developed a prodigious repertory of agonized expressions. But even so I have had to bring in various external props in order to keep the show going. Vases, for example, which can be thrown against a wall at the right moment, and shirts previously weakened by the judicious application of a razor, which can be horribly rent.

Last Tuesday I so far surpassed myself that I have not dared perform since, knowing that whatever I do next will be a letdown. I had hauled a huge Royal office typewriter up from the basement, where it had been rusting for the past ten years. It was a massive piece of machinery, and getting it up the last flight of stairs was a feat in itself. Heaving it at last onto the table, I collapsed in the chair. It took me a few minutes to catch my breath, minutes which I was sure she was using to more precisely focus her instrument. I reflected how this panting collapse, even though perfectly genuine, was a fitting prelude to my performance, a mood-setting overture to the opera that was about to begin. And then I started to type, or pretend to type, since most of the keys had been rendered immobile by rust. I worked hesitantly at first, pecking at the keys with two fingers, pausing to scratch my head, yet gradually increasing the tempo as the creative wheels gained traction. I let the frenzy come on gradually, and yet relentlessly, until finally I stood up, knocking the chair over behind me, and worked standing, hunched over and hammering at the keys. And then, quite precipitously, I stopped, as if assailed by some awful final thought. I momentarily hid my face in my hands. I was overcome by strange grief! I staggered back against the wall, then stumbled forward. I grasped the typewriter in both hands, lifted it high above my head, and taking two running strides, hurled it through the open window. A second or so of exquisite silence ended with a tremendous crash. The machine hit the sidewalk and shattered. Some of the smaller parts flew all the way across the street, ricocheting off the side of a parked car. I turned away, but not before a glance confirmed that she was bouncing wildly in her chair. I ran downstairs and peeked around the edge of my tarp. She had slumped forward in her chair, and for a dreadful moment I thought that I had killed her. But a few seconds later she lifted her head, and I breathed a sigh of relief. I imagined her face streaked with tears.

I am, otherwise, despite my histrionic talents, quite tired of myself. Do you ever have the wish that you were someone else? I would like very much to be someone named Walter Fudge.

Your old friend,
Andy

¶

Dear Mr. Carmichael,

Thank you for Mama's box. I was expecting something much smaller. It is astonishing how much of her there still is. As to your offer of a durable urn in appropriate style, when I looked through your catalogue I was tempted by Grecian Classique Marble and also by Everlasting Bronze, but in the end I have followed your suggestion and just looked around me to see what would harmonize with my furnishings, and I have concluded that the box you sent her in is perfect.

I have your invoice. While I can't send anything right now, I want you to know that I am putting you on top of the pile.

Sincerely,

Andrew Whittaker

¶

Dear Fern,

You and Dahlberg?

I hold my head in my hands and shake it until it laughs. What a jolly melon. And then I try to make it cry, but it can't, since like most old melons it is completely hollow.

When I saw the San Francisco postmark on your letter I thought it was Willy Laport inviting me to Stanford.

I am fascinated that you find San Francisco hilly. But I was not, as you seemed to assume, "interested to learn" that Dahlberg can do a perfect imitation of the call of the sloth. That is *my* nose trick. That he is able to do it using your belly button is irrelevant and revolting. In fact, I can think of nothing which I personally would find more repellant than having a chubby hardware-store clerk wiffle on me, except perhaps having my intimate correspondence read by one. And you are right, I cannot imagine how much fun he is.

Of course I am disappointed that you have thrown away the opportunities I dangled in front of you in order to go live in a truck.

However, I am more disappointed that I am not going to lecture at Stanford.

I wish you both the best.

Your former editor,

Andrew Whittaker

¶

Freewinder!

In your letter—or, rather, in your letters, since they float in one upon the other—you ask if I am "aware" that I have missed several mortgage payments. Rest assured, the awareness of this is like a light burning in my head. Yet even as I admit this awareness, which, as I said, burns like a light in what you, if you were in there with me, would see is a truly terrifying darkness, I would like for you also to become "aware" that I expect to miss even more payments in the future, perhaps gobs, as the saying goes. Hence more light! This is because I am in shit over my head. However, I assure you that the light burning in my head, proudly burning there, will burn brightly even as I and my head and everything burning in it sink from sight.

Sincerely,

Andrew Whittaker

¶

sliced cheese
rolls
mouthwash
t.p.

cans
turkey necks
pig cheeks
chicken backs
what else?
coffee
Crisco
a different life

¶

Dear Jolie,

First it was ants, and now it's mice, or even rats. I can't be sure. I hear them moving around in the walls, making scratching noises, or chewing noises, so it might be either one. I suppose rats would be louder, but because they are inside the walls there's no way of knowing how loud the noise really is. Is that a mouse close up or is that a rat far away? That's a question, I think, which can be asked of almost anything.

The fact is I don't want to do this anymore. All around me things are in decay, or in revolt. If only I could walk out of myself the way one walks out of a house. Good-bye, old pal. Good-bye, old toaster, old sofa, old stack of old magazines. Stand on the stoop, feel the cool breeze coming down the street, feel it blowing through me. Gone at last will be the clogged mess of myself that made me once seem almost solid.

Andy

¶

The sand has become deeper. It is pulverous, like powdered talc. They sink ankle-deep in it; it fills their shoes when they walk. The men and the boys have on socks of black silk, and the sand has infiltrated the cuffs. At first only a little sifted in, but gradually the opening at the top of the cuffs widened as the socks sagged, letting in more sand with each step they take. Now the socks hang in elephantine bulges around their ankles, and they walk with stumbling shuffles like men in shackles. Even the most optimistic among them knows that if the floating things in the river are crocodiles, they will not be able to escape. The women have taken off their shoes. Beneath the long dark dresses with bustles and jabot blouses, they wiggle their toes and remember walking barefoot in Deauville, and they remember how different the sand there was, how course and cool, though in the water there were sharks, concealed, swimming in patient circles beneath the waves. The people, the men and the women, even the most vociferous, are no longer talking. It is clear to everyone that argument is futile, and that the time for communion, if it ever existed, has now passed. The sun has reached the zenith, brilliant, blinding, unbearable. The men have removed their dark coats, dropping them in the sand at their feet. Now they take off their shirts and wrap them around their heads. The women have opened their blouses. They open and close the sides of their blouses, fanning their bare chests. The only shade is cast by the parasols which the women hold just inches above their heads. The children, desperate, perhaps already dying, have crawled under the women's skirts. There in the mysterious dark, like the darkness in the churches at home, they kneel in the sand, and the bare legs of the women, rising up into the strange obscurity above, are like the columns of cathedrals. The men want to draw close to the women, to shrink into the shadows of their parasols, but they do not dare. Even now they do not dare. And when darkness finally comes, and all of consciousness is focused on a single sense, they become aware of the sound of the river behind them, the very faint liquid whispering of water against the bank. They turn, singly, and move toward the sound. The sand reaches above their knees. They struggle through it like travelers floundering in deep snow.

¶

Dear Vikki,

It's all over. I enclose the letter I am mailing out to everyone. I should have done this years ago. I tell myself that, but it doesn't help. I feel emptied out, hollowed and cored. I look into myself and it's like peering into a dry cistern. I shout into it, "Is anybody *down there*?" You can imagine what I get for an answer. I still have a lot of things to do.

Much love,

Andy

¶

Dear Contributor,

We are returning your submission unread. We would have enjoyed reading it, probably, but were prevented doing so by the thought that you doubtless would like it back sooner rather than later, so you can submit it somewhere else, should that be your intention. For, alas, *Soap* is no more. The forces of conformity contrived to starve it of nourishment until it died. It is survived by its editor Andrew Whittaker, who was observed crawling from the wreckage last Friday afternoon and was seen again, several hours later, waving from a bus.

Sincerely,

Walter Fudge,

Executor for the Estate

¶

Dear Jolie,

For the past couple of days, ever since I threw the Royal typewriter, the big gray thing we got from Papa, out the bedroom window, people stop on the sidewalk across the street and point. The police came in three cars and I told them I was typing on the windowsill and it fell out. There is not going to be a Soap Festival. I can't imagine why I ever thought that would be an interesting thing to do. Come to think of it, I am not sure I ever told you about it. No point now.

Andy

¶

Dear Stewart,

I did get the questionnaire and I did fill it out, but I never mailed it, and now it is lost. The inside pocket of my jacket is torn, and I sometimes forget this, and then the things I slip in there vanish for good, unless I happen to hear them hit the ground, which in the case of your questionnaire I am sure I did not. Since it was only one sheet it would not have made much noise anywhere it fell, and I have lately spent a lot of time walking on grass. Furthermore, as we are now in October, a falling questionnaire would have had to compete with the sound of descending leaves aptly described as a rustle.

But losing it was probably for the best, as I have come to have second thoughts about some of my answers. I was, in any case, embarrassed by the condition of the sheet, which bore on its wrinkled surface evidence of once having been tightly balled up. I want you to know that this balling up, if it occurred, was not connected to my feelings about you and Jolie or the things you said about the accident with the vase, but was a result of the state my nerves are in these days and the frustration occasioned by some of your questions. Marital status, for example. There I just had to take a wild guess. Also the question, "Do you consider yourself innocent?" Here we have a question which kept Kafka and Dostoevsky, to name just two, on the mat, not to mention Kierkegaard, and you want *me* to check "Yes" or "No"? I puzzled over that one for hours before hitting on what I thought at the time was a satisfactory solution. But on reflection I now think that checking both boxes was probably more confusing than helpful. And even if I could have settled decisively on one or the other—or even on both or neither—that would still leave the whole question of degree as wide open as ever. I usually think I am thirty percent innocent, but you did not provide any place for that. I don't suppose the judge is going to let me talk about this. Finally, your request that I describe myself in twenty-five words or less has me stumped, though I have made a start.

Andy

¶

Smart aleck

Wiseass

A storm of criticism

A shadow of himself

A blind man in a blind house

A coruscating ape

¶

Adam raised an edge of the window shade. A sliver of after-noon sunlight raced across the room, forcing Fern to lift a slim hand to her face in order to shield her eyes from the impact of the sudden brightness. Adam turned and leaned an elbow on a narrow dresser from which the veneer had begun to peel in jagged strips. He did not need to open the top drawer to know that in it was a Gideon Bible, for this hotel room, with its yellow wallpaper and iron bed, was all the hotel rooms he had ever stayed in. Leaning there, he looked at Fern sprawled on the bed, bisected by the beam, half in light and half in shadow, one arm raised as if to ward off his gaze, while with the other she struggled with something in her lap, and she was all the women he had ever been with. And now he thought of the previous night, and of her in that night, and his mouth, hitherto a resolute crease, twitched merrily at both corners. Fern saw this and smiled wanly, for lack of sleep and an abundance of alcohol had reduced her to a stupor. Chuckling grimly, he turned from her, to peer cau-tiously through the crack at the edge of the shade. For a moment he could see nothing, while his bloodshot eyes adjusted to the glare. Then, as the scene across the street seeped into focus, the chuckles died like strangled marbles in his throat. From the bed Fern could see his whole body heave as if seized by some spasm. She was not surprised, as she also felt queasy. She could not, however, supine as she was at the far end of the room, small though it was, actually glimpse what he was looking at.

This was a low brick building, resembling a warehouse, with STINT BROS. TOWING in white paint above the doorway. The doors were open and Adam could see the back half of a wrecker parked inside, its iron hook hanging from the steel cable like an upside-down question mark. But it was not just this that had caused him to stagger backwards two steps. At the side of the building was a dirt yard, and there he had spotted the familiar remains of his vehicle, the remains of his familiar vehicle, stacked in several neat piles: fenders together in one place, doors in another, the smaller parts in little heaps of their own. And in the midst of them all the once-powerful engine lay on its side in the dirt, wires and tubes cruelly severed, their mutilated stubs sticking up. Adam knew there was no mechanic on earth able to fit those pieces back together, and he cursed himself for having stayed in bed so late, and cursed Fern too for twice dragging him back when he had tried to get up. Dozens of other cars, mostly luxury models in various states of dismantlement, were scattered about among the puddles and dismal weeds that tufted the yard here and there. Around it all ran a high chain-link fence topped by three rows of barbed wire. Adam had seen operations like this before, for he had been an investigator for one of America's leading insurance companies probably, before his life had taken the turn which had brought him to this place, which was as near nowhere as a place can get, and into the arms of this woman, who was now sitting on the edge of the bed trying to get the cap off a vodka bottle. Adam walked over. "This way," he said, showing her which way to turn it. "I know how to fuckin' do it" she slurred irritably.

Adam shrugged and resumed his vigil at the window. His eyes hurt and he was annoyed by the continuing sounds of struggle behind him. And then he saw the dog. It was lying on a car seat in front of a rack of chrome bumpers, concealed, as it were, in their dazzle, and it appeared to be asleep. Adam had mistaken it at first for a large bag of garbage, of which there were indeed many scattered about the yard, one of the most untidy places he had ever witnessed, but now he saw that it was a Doberman pinscher. The animal must have felt his gaze upon it, as dogs are wont to do even as they sleep, for it opened one eye and stared at Adam, who quickly let the shade drop. He turned back to the room. Leaning a pensive elbow on the dresser, he looked at Fern working at the bottle cap with her teeth. He contemplated her smeared lipstick, dirt-streaked face, the bits of straw in her hair, the torn flower-print blouse with sweat stains at the armpits. Then he thought of his wife Glenda in her white tennis shorts, leaping over the net at the end of a vigorous match, her shirt still neatly tucked. His mind reeled.

He slumped, sliding down the wall to the floor, where he sat with his back against the yellow wallpaper, legs outstretched and toes pointing up at the ceiling. Fern wandered over and sat beside him, similarly. From the street below the window rose the babble and clang of a typical small town, the excited cries of children, both joyous and not, mingled with the chatter of townspeople bumping into each other on the streets, as they did every day with equal freshness. From up in the hotel room they sounded like chickens. This caused Fern to think of the farm and the pitiful bunch of vitreous-eyed gallinacae there. She pictured them pecking irritably at bits of gravel, tinfoil, and the filter tips from her father's Tareytons, tossed carelessly this way and that, and she saw them stagger as if inebriated. The tiny eggs, about the size of walnuts, were sprinkled in disorderly patterns about the farmyard, and sometimes the chickens tripped over them; and she pictured that too. Thinking of the chickens made her think ineluctably of her father, for whom the chickens, even though sick, unattractively bald in spots, and feculent, were cherished reminders of his departed wife, who used to call them by clucking on the kitchen steps. She recalled her final glimpse of the old farmer through the rear window of the big truck, little more than a dark smudge in the huge cloud of dust they had churned up behind them. His pathetic questions about the mower hung in her memory.

Was it because their bodies had cleaved in passionate embrace for the past several hours that their minds had so intertwined and fused that Adam too was thinking of chickens? Even as he stared numbly at the yellow wallpaper in front of him, which at that moment seemed to pulsate? For the first time since he had seen the figure crossing from Glenda's bedroom to the beach—an apparition that had propelled him on this ill-fated journey back to the ancestral plot—he let himself imagine another life, one without the tormenting presence of Glenda and Saul, if that apparition had indeed been Saul, which he could never know for sure, or of Glenda and Saul and someone else, in case it had been someone else, as it surely might have been, given the dim light and the possibility, nay, even probability, that what looked like a goatee was really a piece of something hanging from the departing person's mouth, toast or lettuce, for surely Adam's arrival had interrupted the lovers' meal, as was attested by the half-gnawed lamb chops under the table, hurled there obviously in haste. He shook his head violently from side to side in an attempt to drag his mind from this morass, and to imagine another, better, life, one without so many commas. Even as he sat in ungainly abandon, his legs sticking out in front of him, on the floor of the dingy hotel room across the street from Stint Bros. Towing, where he most surely would be going soon, to what end and consequence he knew not, he let his imagination play with the idea of a life shared with Fern on a little chicken farm, clinging, as it were, to this desperate vision as to an inflated inner tube. He imagined sunlight streaming into a modest kitchen and fresh eggs for breakfast.

Fern looked over at Adam and attempted to take his hand in hers, but he drew it back, as if burned. Indeed, he got to his feet. "I'm going to see Dahlberg," he said in a voice of surprising flatness, and stepped to the door. Fern's wide eyes pleaded mutely even as they filled with salty liquid. Then she uttered something, but whether lamentation or warning, he could not tell, for her speech was slurred and indistinct. Tearing his trouser leg from her grasp, tearing it as he tore it, he looked a last time at her upturned face and flung himself from the door, flung himself out the door.

Meanwhile, in a small office at the rear of the garage, Dahlberg Stint sat with his feet up on a large wooden desk. His big brother Tiresome stood behind him, his huge hands hanging at his sides. Dahlberg was eating a sandwich. Though it was lunchtime, Tiresome had no sandwich, for he had consumed his on morning break, as he was wont to do daily despite his oft-uttered resolutions to the contrary, resolutions which he had repeated strenuously to himself that very morning even as he was removing the rubber band and unfolding the wax paper. Dahlberg munched slowly, occasionally lifting the bread to peer inside, thus exposing to Tiresome's gaze the gaudy interior of salami, pickles, tomatoes, and mayonnaise. There was some malice in this, for Dahlberg already knew what was inside. Now he closed the sandwich a final time but did not resume chewing or even swallow what was in his mouth, for he had glimpsed above the crusty rim of the bread the figure of a man silhouetted in the doorway of the garage. Indeed it was the silhouette of a man whose figure was strangely familiar.

He removed his feet from the desk and lowered the sandwich until it rested firmly on the blotter. The bread was white with long black smudges made by Dahlberg's fingers, nail-bitten appendages that he was now wiping briskly against the front of his coveralls, upon which the gaudy entrails of sandwiches from days gone by were thickly spread, for there were no napkins. He shot a quick glance at Tiresome, a glance which said clearly, "There is the figure of a silhouette in the doorway. Be prepared." Tiresome nodded in mute assent, for such was the rapport between the eye-sets of the two, then let his own gaze drop quickly to the sandwich. As he stared at it, half-eaten and isolate in the center of the desk blotter, it seemed to pulsate. In order not to shoot an arm out and snatch it too soon, before he was certain his brother had abandoned it for good, a precipitation which could earn him a rap on the knuckles with a box wrench, he forced his huge hands into the pockets of his coveralls, pockets that were constricted by the prior presence of sundry other items, and so held his hands firmly once he had worked them in there up to the wrists. Dahlberg stood up, if "up" is the word for someone that short, his scrawny neck convulsing as he struggled to swallow the final dry mouthful of sandwich.

Adam crossed the garage, walking carefully to avoid the scattered tools and oily rags, and stepped through the doorway of the office. He looked at the two men standing behind the desk, and he almost smiled. There stood the slack-jawed giant, his dull gaze oscillating between Adam and what appeared to be a piece of moldy sponge on the desk, and next to him, head barely reaching his chest, his brother's chest, was the homely little man with squiggly pig eyes, rotting teeth, and a bad complexion.

"I've come for my car." Adam said.

"What car would that be, mister?" Dahlberg rasped. His voice was like a fly walking on sandpaper. Then he sat down in the chair, from which he had leaped "up" on Adam's entrance, and took hold of the sandwich, as if to casually resume his lunch. He looked up at his brother. "Tiresome, you know anything about this gentleman's car?"

Tiresome blinked vapidly, while Dahlberg casually hoisted the sandwich to his mouth, still looking at his brother. Adam took in the low sloping forehead, the thin upturned nose, and the sandwich slanting downward from the mouth. Recognition hit him like a fist at the same moment that Tiresome's huge right fist, which he had secretly worked free of his pocket, crashed into his, Adam's, face, as it had crashed into the faces of many others since he, Tiresome, was "small."

¶

Dear Harold,

Yesterday I looked out the window and saw that someone had written "asshole" in red paint on my car. And in the midst of everything I forgot to tell you that my mother has died. I had meant to tell you also about some policemen I ran into. Now both will have to wait for another letter. The "Rapid Falls residents living it up at the State Fair" that you see pictured on this postcard are not any people I know. I am convinced their happiness is illusory. That is something I think you should know about me.

Andy

¶

Dear Stewart,

Given the state of my nerves, as cited previously, I have decided it would be a good idea for you to try and postpone this hearing thing. Also the fact that I do not currently have an outfit. I cannot sleep at all these days, in the nights of these days, or even in their afternoons, however emptily they creep, except sometimes on the grass in a few of the city's nicer parks, lulled by the leafy rustling I mentioned in my previous letter. But in most parks I cannot, because the dogs walk on me. I have been writing a lot of letters lately, and I lie awake thinking about them, remembering the old ones and thinking up snappy new ones, and fresh people to write them to. Sometimes I stick them up on the refrigerator with magnets until I can think of someone to send them to. I often revise the old letters in my head, when they need revising, or just think about them with satisfaction when they do not. If they are satisfactory, it is easy to lie quietly in bed, and, though that is not sleeping, it is still something. But it frequently happens that, just as I begin to slide toward sleep, a new idea will charge into my mind, pop in there quick as a wink before I can do anything to stop it, and if it is a good one—and in that state of mental torpor they all seem good ones at first—I then begin to worry that, if I let it out of my mind, tuck it under the pillow, as it were, in order to go on sleeping, it will be forgotten in the morning. So sometimes I force myself to get up. Completely exhausted, I drag myself out of bed and over to the desk to write it down. The result, of course, is that by the time I have finished setting it all down, perhaps tweaking it a little at the corners or correcting some small inconsistency, I am wide awake and there is nothing to be done about it. Faced with that prospect, I sometimes choose a different course. Rather than leaping for a pencil, I stay in bed and say my invention over and over in a soft yet audible voice in the hope of lodging it in my brain so firmly it will still be there in the morning. And sometimes it is. But just as often it is not, and in that case I am left with only the empty fact that I thought something important during the night and have now lost it. Most mornings I don't remember even that much, and in a way that is worst of all, because then I am unable to banish the suspicion that during the night I really did hatch an incredible idea which was subsequently so thoroughly erased while I slept that I don't have any record of its passage. So I lie in bed for hours, torn between a desire for sleep and a hunger to preserve my ideas, either by getting up and writing them down, or by saying them over and over to myself. So equal are these opposing impulses that I am tossed back and forth from one to the other, unable to give in to either, and I wake up, if you can call it waking up, exhausted and irritable. The tragic part of all this is that even when I do succeed in memorizing an idea, or writing it down, it almost invariably proves worthless, its aura of brilliance nothing more than a trick of the half-dreaming state in which even the stupidest and most banal cognitions look like the products of genius.

Your devoted client,
Andy

¶

Dear Vikki,

It is night. Inside that night is another night. This empty house. And the house is not just empty, the emptiness is empty. Outside in the street a siren approaches, passes, fading, becomes an insect, dies. Night, emptiness, but not silence, oh no, not silence. Too cold for crickets, but not for dogs. They bark in relay across the neighborhood, for hours on end. Who can sleep? Who *wants* to sleep? A rumor is going around among the tenants, that because I've been arrested they don't need to pay their rent anymore. God's only excuse, as Stendhal (I think it was Stendhal) said, is that he does not exist. If all else fails, I can go shoot a dog. The notorious Andrew Whittaker, sentenced to death by a jury of dogs, his peers. Write me.

Andy

¶

Dear Dr. Hawktiter,

I was going to send you a little note weeks ago, to thank you for standing up for me in the newspaper. Somehow the note never got written. And now I am writing for a different reason, because you are a medical man and I have developed a strange noise in my head. Of course I don't know if you are that kind of medical man. If you are a podiatrist you will probably be stumped. I suppose I need an ear, nose, and throat man, or even a brain specialist. If you know any of those perhaps you could pass this letter on to them. I hope you will not take this preference amiss in case you specialize in something else. There are so many interesting parts, organs and appendices, also canals of course, that I think it a wonder anyone can decide which way to go, and I certainly don't blame you for making the choice you did. I used to have a leak somewhere, but that seems to have fixed itself. It is possible, however, that it has merely migrated upward and is now responsible for the buzzing sound, even though it was nothing like a buzzing before, in the place it was before. This is not implausible when you consider how the same event can make very different noises in different locations. Take something that, as a podiatrist, you will be familiar with: footsteps in an empty house sound entirely different from the steps made by the same feet, by the feet of the same person, on grass, for example. In the first case we have a kind of hollow knocking which is quite depressing in the long term, while the second is more of a pleasant whisper. I can't render the latter in words exactly but "oopsy-whoosh" seems to come close. It is especially pleasant in autumn, when the fallen leaves chip in their little rustle. Perhaps that is not your view, though. It is difficult to divorce feet from shoes, and this makes the whole discussion almost impossible to conduct in an orderly way, since the different shoe styles and materials, of which there must be hundreds, if not thousands, just mean that there will be that many exceptions to any rule one might come up with. I know that buzzing is a loose term. So many things do buzz. Bees, of course, but also electric fans with things caught in them.

The buzzing I am talking about is very similar to the noise a television I once owned used to make after it had been on for a while. I realize that this will not bring anything to your mind, and hence will not be helpful in forming a diagnosis, unless of course you happen to be one of the men Jolie brought home during that period, and also looked at television with her, which I hardly think any of them ever did. But I believe that what I discovered as a consequence of this resemblance might be quite useful, which was that I could suppress the noise in my head in the same way I got rid of it in the television. In fact, when I experienced the former for the first time about a month ago I immediately thought of using the book trick, and to my surprise it worked like a charm, at least in the beginning. In the case of the TV, though, the fix was only temporary. The intervals without buzzing grew shorter and shorter, and we had to slap it with bigger and bigger books. Toward the end, if I wanted to watch my programs, Jolie had to sit behind the set and bang it with a dictionary every couple of minutes. Of course the banging combined with her grousing was almost worse than the buzzing, and finally I replaced the set with a new Zenith.

Now I am going to tell you about a strange coincidence. Last week I was in the grocery store. I was rummaging in the bin where they keep the bent cans, when I was accosted by a large woman digging next to me. "Hello, there," she said, turning to me with what I thought was a blond leer. I naturally assumed she was making advances, as women will to me, still, but then she introduced me to the man standing behind her. "Charlie," she said, pointing at me, "He's the guy who sold us that TV." And then I knew who she was. The TV she was referring to was the RCA with the buzz. I braced myself for something unpleasant to issue from Charlie, but instead he said, "Best TV we ever owned. Drop it. Leave it out in the rain. Can't kill the little fucker. Wish they made color sets like that." You can imagine my astonishment. I asked, "So the buzzing doesn't bother you?" "What buzzing?" he said. It was then that I remembered I had not told him about that when I sold it, and I stammered out something about the weather we were having lately making my own set buzz. Of course, by my own set I meant my head, though naturally I didn't want to discuss that with them in the grocery store, and in any case weather has nothing to do with it.

The noise has been going on, as I said, for several months. I don't think there is any swelling. I check for this every day, knowing it would be a bad sign. Of course I am not foolish enough to think one can just look in the mirror and tell whether one's head is still the same size. I have a hat which once belonged to my father, which fits me quite snuggly, and I use this as the test. Lately, however, I have begun to wonder whether, by dint of pulling the hat on and off several times a day, I might be stretching it. So there could be some undetected swelling. I once had a doctor measure my head to see if it was the right size, the size of other people my size, with bodies my size, and he used an enormous pair of calipers. I suppose using a hat will strike you as incredibly amateurish.

I am writing you now because I sense that things are approaching a climax. Two nights ago I was on Seventh Street on my way back from a park, when I stopped in front of Little

Champion Sporting Goods to look at the display in the window. It was just football equipment, jerseys, helmets, and the like, and did not interest me in the slightest. The noise had been getting worse ever since I had left the park, and I was cursing myself for having forgotten to bring along a book. Even a small paperback will usually do the trick, and I had always carried one in my hip pocket until that ripped. Not having a book I tried the flat of my hand to no effect. I was surprised at how feeble the blow was. I suppose it was the sight of the football equipment that prompted me to think of butting. Of course I should have moved over a few feet to where the concrete wall was, but by that time I was feeling really quite desperate, and so, in the throes of that desperation, I butted my head against the glass. It did not seem to me that I was butting very hard at all, it was not hurting to any real extent, and yet on the third or forth blow a silver line slithered up the glass from the bottom left, passed in front of my eyes, and raced to the opposite corner. It made a dreadful, dry, tearing noise as it went. I turned and began to run down the street. I had not taken two steps when the whole window crashed to the sidewalk. It was two a.m., there were only a couple of people on the street, and in the silence the sound of the breaking glass seemed deafening.

I am aware that the glass incident is not medically significant, but I bring it up as an illustration of how fed up I am with this noise. When I hold my head in my hands, as I do often these days, I can feel it bombinate. Perhaps the cause is something simple, even humdrum, and you could recommend a medication. I have thought of trying yoga but I am not sure being upside down is a good idea, especially when I consider that there may be a leak involved. Just thinking about it produces horrible images of stuff running out everywhere.

Your author in distress,
Andrew Whittaker

¶

Dear Jolie,

Yesterday I was at the opening of Stanley's show at the Downtown Gallery—a place where I am sure no one expected to see me—and I found myself on a sofa next to Billy Kippers, to whom I have not spoken a civil word in years. He was chatting with the Simms woman, who was sitting next to him on the other side. In the midst of all the noise I couldn't overhear much of what they were saying, but I caught her stealing glances in my direction, so I presumed the worst. I refrained from sticking my tongue out, because I had promised Stanley I would behave. After a while the Simms creature left, and Billy turned to me. Resting a hand on my shoulder and inclining his head close to mine he asked, in almost a whisper, "How's the novel going?" I was so surprised that at first I couldn't think what to answer. I suspected malice. But when I looked in his face, into that porcelain-pale dinner-plate of a face with its blue unblinking gaze, he seemed *concerned*. I stammered out something to the effect that it was going great guns. I was so affected by his question that I thought for a moment I was going to cry real tears. I wonder what he would have thought if I had laid my head on his shoulder and sobbed?

I have been saying to myself, Perhaps there is someone who will. But then I ask myself, Is there anyone who can?

Something has been falling from the sky. It could be snow. It could be tears. It could be the chain of days. Imagine, the chain of days falling like snow! What would that look like? The fact is, somewhere there is something, as I have been saying to myself repeatedly. But not really. Whittaker, what are you doing in there? is what I have really been saying for a long time. I have said it over and over, but no one has answered. That is because I was whispering it. It sounded like shouting to me. In here it is horribly loud, but out there it is not even a whisper. What is less than a whisper? Too terrible to think.

I have no plans. I don't remember a time before when I had no plans. I wander from room to room and kick things. I lie on the sofa and imagine that I am covered in fur.

In front of me I see a blankness. I don't know if it is an open door or a wall. I don't know how to find out. Do you have any suggestions? I think I am going to stop now.

Andy

p.s. If in the envelope with the suggestions, you could slip a few dollars . . .

¶

Dear Willy,

You have failed to answer my previous letters, but as you can see I have not given up. For most of my life I have been dragged down by ideas of dignity, vanity really, and a strong desire to be liked. However, I suspect that this is all behind me now, or else how could I bring myself to write you again after the indifference and contempt conveyed by the absence of even a postcard from you? I regard this change in my outlook as a breakthrough. A breakthrough and a blessing, that's what it is. I used to cringe whenever I pictured you looking up from one of my missives and saying to someone, perhaps to a room full of female students, "Listen to this, girls." And then you read aloud a few choice passages from my letters in a high, simpering voice, while the young things bite their lips to hide the mirth occasioned by your hideous rendition of my desperate plight. I had only to imagine the eventual outbreak of overt tittering for a hot flush of shame to o'erspread my neck and face. I am writing to let you know that it doesn't matter now: I have unpacked my soul and there is nothing in it.

And speaking of packing, I don't know if I wrote you about my boxes. Last month I was very busy putting up in cardboard cartons almost everything I owned that might be called personal, even at a stretch. I started with just a few things I didn't need at the moment, and gradually accelerated. In the end I had packed everything except the furniture and appliances, which were too big, and a change of clothes. As I folded down the flaps of each box and taped them shut, I experienced a very small impulse of joy. It was little more than a twinge, but after doing a series of boxes I sometimes felt giddy and had to lie down, which leads me to suppose that the impulses, small as they were, are accumulating somewhere, perhaps to burst forth some day in the future. There were soon a lot of boxes, and I found it difficult to move about in the living room, where I had most of them stacked. In fact, I had to choose at any given moment whether I wanted access to the front door, the upstairs, or the kitchen. I found myself spending much too much time moving boxes, even though I did, at first, enjoy experimenting with different arrangements. I also for a while enjoyed building towers so high and so precariously tottering that I could make them fall over just by jumping up and down in increasingly distant places in the house, eventually getting as far away as the kitchen. But when that became boring, as it quickly did, I started getting rid of them. The odd thing is, when I first packed the boxes it was with the intention of just putting things aside, getting them out from under foot, so to speak. It had not yet entered my head that I could get rid of them altogether and permanently. Yet this now became my all-consuming goal. Fearing that a large number of boxes thrown out at one time would provoke objections from the pick-up men, especially since the majority were full of books and extremely heavy, I had to carry out the project gradually, stealthily in a sense, at a rate of eight or nine cartons a week. Thursdays are garbage days. I think of them as blessed garbage days. In the early morning I would stack at the curb as many boxes as I dared. Then I would go and sit at an upstairs window to wait for the truck. Every box was labeled, the contents listed in minute detail, so I knew exactly what things were about to embark. Every collection day brought a small thrill—even saying good-bye forever to something as insignificant as a pair of socks was something—but the moment of supreme joy arrived the day all my writing, everything up to the moment I started packing a few months ago, took the ride. Notebooks, manuscripts, scribbles great and small. Seven boxes of it. In the remaining four boxes going out that morning I had been careful to place only the least interesting objects, so as not to mar the singularity of that day's pleasure. The collectors were the usual pair of big-gloved ex-convicts. When they pitched the boxes into the truck, I nearly fainted with glee. I watched the hydraulic crusher close over them. It whined as it mashed them in with other people's most prosaic trash, garbage, leftovers, and other ejections, pulping it all into a varicolored sludge. I was sorry that there was no way for me to get inside and watch.

Having witnessed my belongings and achievements embarking in this way, I have thought that perhaps I should imitate them. Of course I can't hope to literally put myself into a compactor. I could, however, just take a trip. I am not sure about my car, though. It seems to me an untrustworthy item. It stops for no apparent reason, often in the middle of an intersection, and refuses to go on. Then, just when I have decided to get out and cajole a push from the vehicle behind me (which at this point has begun to honk), when I have already one foot on the pavement, it will suddenly leap forward, forcing me to scramble back in or be left sitting in the roadway. I used to be embarrassed by this, but since my breakthrough I just wave gaily as I shoot off. On the other hand, the car starts without fail in the cold and seems likely to run for a while once I have coaxed it up to speed on the highway, and a while is plenty of time to get there. Get where? you ask, and well you should. After all, getting somewhere must be the point of it all, else why embark? And that is really the question I keep asking myself. Why embark at all? I could just as well stay where I am, on my sofa or in my deck chair if I feel like it, or on the grass in the park. But it will soon be getting too cold for that, and then it will have to be on the snow in the park. Just thinking of this makes me wonder if I shouldn't put off my embarkation for a month or so, in order to be able to lie down in the snow in the park. Above me the stars will be icy pinpricks in the clear blackness of the winter sky. The branches of the oaks will be blacker still. The idea of a further journey will naturally occur to me then, there in the snow, but I shall not let myself be tempted. I know myself well enough to suppose that I won't stay out that long, long enough to really embark. No, I imagine I'll stay out just long enough to catch a nasty cold. As all the reward for my effort I'll have ten days of dripping nose and soggy Kleenex. However, I also know it is really just the enormous appeal which adventure has always held for me that seduces me into imagining I will be able to get even that far. In fact I will probably not succeed even in getting out the door. I'll open it, a blast of cold air will rush in, and that will be enough to do the trick. I'll shiver and think, Not now.

But the idea doesn't leave me, and a few minutes later I am back at the door. With all my things finally gone, it is really only a matter of time. You see, there is nothing for me to do here anymore. I am embarking because I am bored, because I am frightened, because I am sad. But really because I don't find my jokes funny anymore. Looking back over them I ask myself if they were ever funny, or did I just make them seem so by my laughter.

Your faithful correspondent,
Andrew Whittaker

¶

COLOPHON

The Cry of the Sloth was designed at Coffee House Press, in the historic
Grain Belt Brewery's Bottling House near downtown Minneapolis.
The text is set in Iowan Old Style.

FUNDER ACKNOWLEDGMENTS

Coffee House Press is an independent nonprofit literary publisher. Our books
are made possible through the generous support of grants and gifts from many
foundations, corporate giving programs, state and federal support, and through
donations from individuals who believe in the transformational power of literature. Coffee House receives major general operating support from the
McKnight Foundation, the Bush Foundation, from Target, and from the
Minnesota State Arts Board, through an appropriation by the Minnesota State
Legislature and from the National Endowment for the Arts. Coffee House also
receives support from: three anonymous donors; Abraham Associates; the
Elmer L. and Eleanor J. Andersen Foundation; Allan Appel; Bill Berkson; the
James L. and Nancy J. Bildner Foundation; the Patrick and Aimee Butler Family
Foundation; the Buuck Family Foundation; the law firm of Fredrikson & Byron,
PA.; Jennifer Haugh; Anselm Hollo and Jane Dalrymple-Hollo; Jeffrey Hom;
Stephen and Isabel Keating; Robert and Margaret Kinney; the Kenneth Koch
Literary Estate; Allan & Cinda Kornblum; Seymour Kornblum and Gerry
Lauter; the Lenfestey Family Foundation; Ethan J. Litman; Mary McDermid;
Rebecca Rand; Debby Reynolds; the law firm of Schwegman, Lundberg,
Woessner, PA.; Charles Steffey and Suzannah Martin; John Sjoberg; Jeffrey
Sugerman; Stu Wilson and Mel Barker; the Archie D. & Bertha H. Walker
Foundation; the Woessner Freeman Family Foundation; and many other gener-
ous individual donors.

This activity is made possible
in part by a grant from the
Minnesota State Arts Board,
through an appropriation by the
Minnesota State Legislature
and a grant from the National
Endowment for the Arts.

NATIONAL
ENDOWMENT
FOR THE ARTS

MINNESOTA
STATE ARTS BOARD

TARGET.

To you and our many readers across the country,
we send our thanks for your continuing support.

Good books are brewing at www.coffeehousepress.org

Dear Mrs. Lessep,

Thanks for letting us read, once again, "The Mistletoe's Little Shoes." After careful consideration, we have concluded that this work still does not meet our needs. I am sorry you were misled by the phrase "does not meet our needs at this time" into thinking you should submit it again. In the publishing world "at this time" really means "forever."

A. Whittaker, Editor at *Soap*

---

*What happens to us
either happens to everyone or only to us:
in the first instance it's banal;
in the second it's incomprehensible.*
—FERNANDO PESSOA

Dear Bob, Eric, and Juan,

I have received another complaint about the noise. You will have to turn it down after 10 or find another place. Wear clothes when you go to the basement with your laundry. Think of the people in the other apartments, who are not as young as you are, have to get up and go to work, and are religious to boot. None of that is their fault.

Sincerely,
Andrew Whittaker
The Whittaker Company

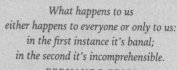

SOAP MAGAZINE
Rapid Falls, USA

Mr. Norman Mailer
New York, NY

---

paint thinner

tile mastic

ant poison

garbage can

interior white

I write like
my mother

post office

light bill

courthouse

pills

stay home

read

go somewhere

so. comfort

food

DIARY ENTRY—

Smart aleck

Wiseass

A storm of criticism

A shadow of himself

A blind man in
a blind house

A coruscating ape

ENJOY A FAMILY LIFESTYLE!
73 Charles Court. Unique single-family bungalow-style house in desirable neighborhood. 2 bdrm 1 bath. Large closets. Security fence. Paved yard. Lighted parking. 10-min walk to shops and gas station. $155 + utils.

PLACE ALL TRASH IN METAL RECEPTACLES
LOCATED AT THE BACK OF THE BUILDING

ATTENTION ALL TENANTS: IF YOU HAVE MISPLACED YOUR MAILBOX KEY, CONTACT PHELPS IN 1A. SHE HAS A MASTER KEY AND WILL RETRIEVE YOUR MAIL. DO NOT TRY TO PRY THE BOXES OPEN!